Return of the Warrior

By Katherine E. Standell
aka Archangel

ISBN 0-9744037-5-X

Second Printing 2003
Cover art and design by L.J. Maas
Back Cover by Anne Clarkson

Published by:
Dare 2 Dream Publishing
A Division of Limitless Corporation
Lexington, South Carolina 29073

Find us on the World Wide Web
http://www.limitlessd2d.net

Printed in the United States of America and internationally by

Lightning Source

Dedication:

To my parents whom I love dearly, and to my soulmate, who knows she holds my heart. I also dedicate this to all the courageous women warriors, past and present. Thank you for breaking the trail.

CHAPTER 1

It was an average early afternoon in Marietta, Georgia. Hot but not too hot, sunny, but not too bright and for a January in Georgia it was kind of nice.

Yep, just your average day and I am going buggy. Dylan sat, thinking and staring out the window; this was the fourth "Welcome Home" ceremony she had attended in as many weeks. She was happy to be back in the United States, but she wasn't thrilled that she had somehow become the ambassador of goodwill for the entire US Army.

Her orders were to follow a schedule of appearances while in route to her home in North Carolina. This obviously included stopping at every major town between Washington, DC and Cherokee, in the Carolinas. The politicians were milking her experience for all it was worth.

Initially, she had not minded, after all the end result was that she was going home and had been given four months of R and R to decide what she wanted to do with her future. Uncle Sugar was anxious to keep her on active duty, but Dylan had been an unwilling civilian now for a three years and she was not sure if she could go back to the rigors and restrictions of the military. Her former Commander, Colonel Fowler had spoken to her personally and had urged her to take the time and really consider her options. That was precisely what she had planned to do, but so far her mind had been preoccupied with speeches and polite political bullshit as she shook hands with mayors and Governors, all eager to be seen with a female combat hero.

Yes, at first it had been a bit exciting, but the constant repeated oration of her experiences was beginning to really trouble her. She had not actually realized how many people's lives she had directly affected. Now she heard it every day and the numbers seemed to get bigger each time she heard it.

Rubbing her temples she turned away from the sunny, perfect view. The normalcy of all the activity seemed to be giving her a painful headache.

It was so strange watching people drive freely up and down the streets, going about their mundane lives. They had no idea what it was like to be amazed and relieved that you woke up each morning. The idea of hunting for food and water or fighting to keep your children alive and your woman from being raped would never occur to those strangers walking in the streets below. Sometimes she felt as if she had been on a different planet and had finally been rescued and beamed aboard the mother ship.

She watched in amazement as people performed the simple acts that made up their daily lives like crossing the street at the crosswalks, pulling into gas stations and fast food places or chatting on the phone while they drove to and from work. That was one activity that she really had a hard time with. Sometimes she still expected to turn a street corner and see the market with the foods hanging in the open air, flies buzzing around it while a small child lazily waved a fan to deter them. Now it seemed like that last three years had all been a horrible dream and she had finally waken to find herself in her own bed…almost.

Thinking again of her location, she was amazed that she was still "on tour". *You'd think the country would be tired of hearing my name.*

She stared around at the huge, cream-colored room where their escort had left them. A beautiful cherry wood table graced the center of the room, its claw toed legs seemed to clutch at the thick blood red carpet. Tall ladder-back matching chairs were scattered in strategic locations against the walls. The standard patriot prints were displayed in matching imitation cherry wood frames. It was all a bit heavy, but overall, the county courthouse was really quite beautiful.

They had already put in their appearance with the Governor and were only waiting on their driver in order to leave. Being use to the vastness of the desert Dylan found staying in the large room uncomfortable. She felt trapped. Unable to remain still and craving the open space of the outdoors, she turned again to stare out the window. She and Lura had arrived earlier that morning and reporters had surrounded the duo immediately, bombarding them with questions and the glaring lights of cameras. Looking down into the street below Dylan could see the limo that had been assigned to them for the duration of their visit. It sat patiently outside and she sorely wished they were in it now. With a deep sigh of resignation she turned to glance at her roommate, slash fellow captive, in all this confusion. Lura sat staring at her folded hands, her hair was dulled and her skin was pale from their extended stay in the hospital following their rescue. Since they had returned from Europe they had had very little time alone and even less in the fresh air and daylight, at least not unescorted. It seemed they were the new stars of the camera and their every movement was top headline news.

She looked closer at her lover and noticed the dark circles under her eyes and the dazed look on her face; exhaustion was evident in the slump of her shoulders.

My poor little falcon looks lost she thought.

Dylan smiled gently at the small blonde; Lura had stuck by her through all the stress and strain of the physical rehab and the mental anguish of reliving and retelling the events in the debriefing session and in front of the crowds at the ceremonies. She had also relived the assault and the death of her friends over and over again.

When they had first arrived back in the States, Lura had suffered from nightmares, calling out in her sleep. Dylan had waken her and held her through those horrible times. They often found themselves making love in an almost desperate frenzy trying to wipe the memories from their minds. Finally, the dreams had stopped. Dylan thought it might have been because Lura had been lucky enough to have closure.

When they had recovered enough to answer questions, Dylan had told the investigators about the camera crew and had given them the coordinates for the destroyed terrorist camp. The remains of Lura's friends had been recovered and given a respectful burial. They had attended the funerals, both were at Arlington and the men were buried as heroes for their actions in the terrorist camp. Following the funeral Lura had cried all night, but afterward the nightmares were gone. Dylan envied her; she had not been around when her men at the camp had been recovered all those years ago. Because of the location of their rescue, the recovery and burial of the remains from the cave had occurred while she was still in the hospital. Her last memories of her men were of the skeletal remains she had been forced to crawl over when she had gone back into the cave for her radio. Now it seemed that every time she entered a closed, dark room she was back in the cave, surrounded by the bones of the dead.

Shaking her head in an effort to drive the morbid thoughts from her mind, Dylan stared again at her lover. Lura was exhausted; that was apparent in the dull glazed look in her eyes and the slight pallor of her cheeks.

"This was the last one, Lura. No more. We're going home."

Lura lifted exhausted but smiling eyes and sighed. "We will do whatever it takes Dylan, but to tell ya the truth, home sounds really, really good right now. I think I could use the break." Slowly she stood stretching her tired body and walked to Dylan, wrapping her arms around the slim waist of the soldier.

Dylan raised her dark blue uniform-clad arms and placed them on the shoulder of her soulmate. Smiling gently down into the soft green eyes, she felt herself relax.

"How do you do it Lura? Just a touch, just a sigh and I turn into a neatly pressed and starched, dress blue uniformed wuss." She smiled, happy to think of more pleasant thoughts.

"Hmm, must be love, sweetheart," came the warm, muffled reply from somewhere deep in the front of her blue jacket.

Lura pulled back far enough to glance up at the beautiful soldier she held in her embrace. She was so proud of her woman, her Hawk. Dylan looked incredibly regal in her Army dress blue uniform. The brass buttons glittered against the dark blue jacket and three rows of multi colored ribbons graced her left breast. The incredible star-studded, deep blue ribbon of the Medal of Honor lay gently nestled against the stark white of her uniform blouse. The medal had been awarded the day she had arrived back in the United States and Lura still remembered the ceremony.

They had arrived at the White House in the early morning. It was still gray outside and the security lights around the huge building glittered off the dew on the lawn. Huge ancient oak trees lined the drive, each one like a gnarled guardian. A police escort, sirens blasting, had taken them straight to the front door of the palatial estate.

Their car doors were opened by their assigned security. They were assisted out of the car and through the front doors into the home of the leader of the most powerful nation on earth.

Lura was concerned about her partner. The injuries they had both suffered had not quite healed and they were exhausted. Dylan was even more so after having withstood a grueling debriefing the day before. She had been through so much already which included months of rehabilitation just to reach the point where she could move under her own power again. Though the tall soldier had healed quickly, the injuries had taken a lot out of her. What really concerned Lura was that, while she had suffered nightmares and depression, Dylan had seemed to deal with it all. She had been understanding, strong and patient, holding her through the worst of it, and often staying up through the long nights just talking. Through it all though, Dylan had not shed a single tear.

They were escorted inside the main foyer where a Secret Service Agent stood with a wheelchair at the ready. She quickly rolled it forward towards Dylan, but stopped when her eyes met the icy daggers of the woman in blue.

Smiling silently, Lura remembered how it had taken her a good ten minutes of arguing to talk the damn stubborn woman into sitting in the chair even though it was obvious to her that the soldier was ready to pass out on her feet. Dylan finally agreed to the chair but only if Lura offered to push it.

With a tired smile she had settled into the padded chair and, motioning forward, had ordered, "Onward, McDuff."

Lura had leaned forward and whispered into one creamy ear. "Now I'm McDuff? Damn, close your eyes for a nap in a military hospital and see what happens. That's the last time I do that." Her comment had been answered by a gentle rumbling chuckle from the chair.

Lura rolled them towards an indicated door where they exited the building and entered the plush grandeur of the South Lawn. A platform, with a wheelchair ramp, stood at the edge of the manicured grass, the podium on it bearing the seal of the President of the United States.

When they had settled into their assigned seats on the platform the doors opened again to admit the viewing public, those that had been invited specifically for the ceremony. Lura saw the man from the cave again, the one who claimed to be her love's father. She felt Dylan stiffen as their eyes met. Senator Cameron assisted his wife, a beautiful dark haired woman, to her seat then turned and climbed the stairs to his daughter. Dylan began to struggle in her chair to rise and face her father but was stopped by a gentle hand on her arm. She turned and looked into a pair of pleading green eyes. Resigned to having to stay seated, she sat up and leaned forward, her hands gripping the arms of the chair. Lura expected a low growl to emanate from the tight throat and was genuinely surprised when it did not.

Dylan waited for the man to speak. He stopped directly in front of her chair and stared down into eyes that mirrored his own. Kneeling in front of the injured woman he bowed his head as if in deep thought then raised his eyes and spoke.

"Dylan, when your unit was attacked and you were reported lost three years ago, I made a promise to God." He paused, catching his breath. "I promised that if he were to give me another chance, just one, to have my daughter back I would do everything in my power to work things out. When we couldn't find you, when you were reported dead..." He stopped, his eyes filled with tears and he reached out blindly for her hands. Grasping them in his as if to draw strength and reassure himself of her existence, he cleared his throat and continued.

"When you were reported dead, I made it my life's work to understand your lifestyle and try to find a way to come to terms with it. I did a lot of reading, I attended meetings and most importantly, I spoke with your Grandfather. I am still not real sure of it all, but I can understand that love comes in a lot of different forms and you don't always have choices about who you love or why. I understand that there is no shame in love and most of all I understand that God does not make mistakes. I have waited three years to ask you one question." He stopped here and looked deep into confused blue eyes.

"Please, please, can you forgive me?"

Dylan stared into the tear-streaked face of her father, then lowered her head and shook it side to side. "I don't know, I don't know," she mumbled. "I need time to think. Please, give me time."

Standing, her father dropped his gaze to his shoes and nodded. What had he expected? He had treated her badly and deserved nothing more. He was still amazed that her mother had taken him back after his reprehensible behavior. He knew his daughter was right; she needed time and so did he. This would be quite an adjustment, first finding her alive and then nearly losing her again, and finally meeting the woman she loved. He had promised God anything for a second chance to be a part of Dylan's life. God had fulfilled his part of the bargain, now he had to give Dylan the freedom to choose if that was what she wanted as well. He would wait, forever if necessary. He would wait. With a slight nod, he rose and returned to his seat.

Dylan turned as her gaze following the tall man and finally settled on the figure of her mother. She looked beautiful and distraught. They had spoken at length on the phone from her recovery room in the hospital, but this was their first face to face in six years.

There was a bit more gray in her hair but her features were still stunning. Her dark eyes were fixed on the activity on the elevated stage; a small frown was all that marred the beauty of her still line-free face. Her mother had always been a quiet shadow in her life and she had never really realized how beautiful she was until that moment. Her father had been a fool to abandon such a woman and his only child. Dylan had a lot to think about. With a shake of her head she redirected her gaze to a third figure.

Following her lover's gaze, Lura could see where Dylan had gotten her incredible looks, but it was the figure behind the couple, the same figure Dylan now stared at, that caught her eye. A tall gray haired warrior sat proudly beside the senator's wife, the copper skin tones enhanced by the almost white buckskin shirt and pants.

Dylan's Grandfather, Gray Hawk, War Chief of the Southern Cherokee, had come to witness the ceremony honoring his granddaughter. He was stunning and proud in his traditional Native American regalia. His thick gray hair had been combed back into two heavy braids that were tied off with leather wraps. A single eagle feather had been braided into one and lay on his chest like a badge of honor. The bone and stone beads that adorned the shirt formed a screaming hawk with talons outstretched. His decorated buckskin pants and leather moccasins glittered the early morning light. In his gnarled hands he held a tall staff decorated with beautiful stones and the names of animals.

Lura watched as his alert black eyes turned to gaze proudly at his granddaughter. Again she felt the shoulder under her hand stiffen, but this time in pride. Dylan seemed to sit up taller; her head rose higher and a bit of the old sparkle appeared in her eyes when they met those of the old man. In turn the gray haired warrior threw his shoulders back and puffed his chest out with pride as a smile appeared on the wrinkled face. Lura now knew where her mate had acquired her courage.

They all settled into padded chairs in front of the podium and within minutes the ceremony began. Lura vaguely remembered the introduction of the Secretary of War who read the citation out aloud for the hungry eyes of the nation's premier news stations. Her eyes were on the President as she walked to the microphone to address the nation. She spoke of the boundless courage of a young Captain, alone in the desert facing insurmountable odds, of her battle with a ruthless enemy who had made it his mission in life to destroy for his own benefit. She told of those last days in the cave and the firefight that ended in the death of "an enemy of humanity" and the horrendous injuries suffered by this "defender of freedom". The President, moved by her own speech, had tears in her eyes as she turned and called Captain Dylan Hawke to the podium.

Lura stood to roll the chair forward, but was stopped by a raised hand. She looked on as the woman she loved slowly struggled from the chair; her pale shaking features telling of the strain that simple action was taking on her.

Lura remember again, the way the uniform hung loosely on the tall frame and the way the soldier swayed gently as she valiantly fought to stay on her feet.

The warrior stepped forward and bowed her proud dark head to allow the President of the United States to lay the Medal of Honor around her neck. It was the reward and thank you for a job well done, from the people of a grateful nation.

Though she was there in the final days, Lura still had not been able to grasp the full enormity of Dylan's accomplishment until that moment. She had survived for three long grueling years virtually alone in the desert and had caused serious damage to an enemy of the United States in the process.

Lura would always remember every moment, every smell and every feel of that day.

CHAPTER 2

The cameras loved the tall dark haired hero and were constantly focusing on the beautiful, haggard face and brilliant blue eyes. That face had graced the cover of more than one magazine over the last month and the demands on her lover's time were as taxing on Lura as they were on the soldier.

Today Lura noticed the sunken cheeks and shaking hands. Dylan had not quite recovered from the extensive surgery that had removed several bullets from her beautiful body. She occasionally complained of what she called 'twinges' that woke her in the night. She had told Lura that the aches and pains were what had forced her to restlessly pace the floor of the hotels.

Lura had watched as Dylan tossed and turned night after night. The journalist knew it wasn't just the injuries; it was the also the nightmares that came from the deep horrid memories of the last three years. The nightmares woke Dylan in a shaking, cold sweat night after long night.

Lura glanced at the ribbon around Dylan's neck, thinking of the real meaning behind the star shaped bit of metal. It didn't just represent the pain and suffering her mate had been through, she knew that it also represented servicemen and women who had willingly placed the lives of others ahead of their own. Ordinary people, who at some point, were called on to do the extraordinary, people who had willingly sacrificed all for the survival of others. These were the few who were awarded the country's highest honor. She also knew that most recipients received the award posthumously.

As they toured the sites of Washington DC with their entourage of security and cameras, she had been amazed to notice the reaction of military personnel. Even general officers saluted the young Captain first when they noticed the ribbon around her neck. They would stop, snap to attention and render a sharp salute that Dylan returned just as sharply. When Lura asked her about it, Dylan shyly replied that they were saluting in respect of the ribbon, its recipient and all those who had gone before.

Squeezing the waist again, Lura felt as if her heart would burst from pride whenever she saw her mate in uniform, *Boy, they were right when they said a woman couldn't resist a soldier in uniform. Oh Boy, were they right!*

Drawn again from her view out the window, Dylan glanced down at the other woman. As she watched, a slow satisfied smile brightened her face as Lura attempted to burrow even deeper into the front of her blue-black jacket, inhaling deeply then sighing gently in contentment. She wondered what had brought on the sudden change. Whatever it was, she was grateful. She had been worried that it had all been too much on her soulmate.

Lura, feeling the warmth of the gaze, glanced up again to the still pale cheeks. The drawn expression told it all. Dylan was barely holding it together and Lura knew it. *Time for a break. I'm gonna get my woman away from all this' and let her unwind before the super glue she is using to hold herself together wears off.* Nuzzling back into the deep blue coat, Lura sighed again. She knew that to address the issue of her concern or to point out any weakness would only upset the soldier. There was only one way to approach this.

"Dylan, I don't know about you, but I really need a break. Is there anyplace we can go and just be... well, normal?"

Dylan looked deeply at her companion and as a slow smile crept across her face, one sable eyebrow raised and the sparkle returned.

"I know just the thing," she said chuckling. Taking her companion's hand, she led her out the door.

Dylan was tired of waiting. *That cussed driver is probably out smoking. Well, too damn bad. We are out 'a here.* Long strides took her across the room where she slowly cracked open the door and cautiously peeked out. The hallway was empty save for a few scattered copies of the same ladder back chairs as in their 'prison'.

Grabbing Lura's small hand in her own she stepped out into the hall. Quickly striding down the corridor and past a startled security guard, Dylan reached the limo. Opening the passenger door she helped Lura in then ran around to the driver's door just as the first reporter raised the alarm.

Smiling with wicked glee, she locked the doors and started the car. Glancing back over her shoulder, she slipped it into reverse and eased the large car through the crowd of flashing bulbs, out into traffic and down the road. The squeal of tires a peal of laughter and the gray puff of exhaust were all that lingered in the air.

On reaching the hotel, Dylan retrieved their key

from the front desk and led Lura to their room. As the blond watched with a bemused expression on her face, her partner unlocked the door, pulled the smaller woman in and snapped the D*o Not Disturb* sign on the outside knob. She locked the door, pushed the dead bolt home, and slipped the chain on. She walked quickly to the window and drew the curtains shut after which she turned and pulled Lura into a bone-crushing hug. "Sometimes you have just the best ideas," she mumbled into the soft blonde hair. "Let's change, then I am going to take you out for the most normal food you have ever eaten."

Quickly changing, Lura and Dylan escaped the confines of the five star hotel the state had paid for and were searching for what Dylan referred to as one of her many "vices". She absolutely had to have a large order of McDonalds' French fries.

"I'm not sure how they make 'em, but, as every true fry connoisseur knows, McDonalds makes the best French fries. Not too hard on the outside, nice and soft on the inside, with just the right amount of salt," Dylan had assured Lura.

Lura knew exactly how much salt Dylan considered "just the right amount." She noticed that the tall woman had a love for the seasoning and tended to overdo it just a bit in that area.

Having gotten directions from the front desk, the two women walked three blocks down the street and into the nearby McDonald's. Minutes later they were seated quietly in a corner booth, munching on crisp hot French fries and slurping down their drinks. Neither noticed the arrival of the news van or the cheerful reporter who stood outside talking to the television camera.

Dylan felt the disturbance first and raised her head. Still munching on a, heavily salted, golden crispy fry, she watched from her corner seat as the other customers began pointing and chatting in excited voices.

"Uh oh," she moaned. Reaching over she place a hand on top of Lura's head, turning her towards the window.

"Oh my. Oh no. Not here," Lura groaned, watching as the perky anchorwoman motioned her cameraman towards the silent couple.

Was I really like that before I met Dylan? YUCK! Lura thought with disgust.

"I am not giving one more God blessed interview," Dylan growled. "All I want is to eat my fries in peace. Make them go away, Lura," she whined, presenting Lura with a pitiful puppy dog pout.

Lura stared into the big blue eyes of her companion and nodded her head. "I'll take care of it baby, don't you worry. I won't let those big bad nasty news people near you," she said in the perfect Mommy voice. "You just sit here and finish your fries, I'll be right back." She stood up, dusted the salt and fry crumbs from her jeans, pulled her shirt straight and headed toward the camera crew. There was a look of staunch determination on her face.

"Go get 'em girl," Dylan mumbled, smiling as she munched on another salty treat.

Holding up her hands to stop any further advance towards her partner, Lura began to speak. "Miss Hawke is not giving any more interviews today. If you have any questions, you may speak with her attorney."

"Are you Lura Grant?" the perky reporter asked,

sweeping past Lura's upraised hands. "How does it feel to be nominated for the Pulitzer Prize?"

"Whaaa? Huuu…? I'm not …but, the Pulitzer Prize?" Lura stammered. Suddenly she felt strong hands lightly grasping her shoulders, turning her back towards the corner booth.

"Miss Grant is not giving any more interviews today. If you have any further questions, you may speak with her attorney. Thank you," Dylan said. She turned and ushered the still stammering, confused blonde back to their table leaving the reporter to stare open mouthed at their retreating backs.

"The Pulitzer? The Pulitzer. B..b..b..but…the Pulitzer." Those were the only words that Dylan could hear from her companion as she guided the still mumbling woman down the aisle, ignoring the stares of the other customers.

Finally reaching their seats, she pushed the stunned journalist down into the booth and slid in next to her. She picked up a French fry and placed it into Lura's hand, guiding the small hand to her mouth just as the words, "The Pulitzer" spilled out again.

Dylan watched the news crew packing up and the frustrated reporter waiving her arms as her camera crew silently ignored her tirade. Turning back to watch the dazed, mumbling blonde, Dylan picked up on the conversation of a couple standing in line next to them. A petite, smiling woman stood next to a tall young man. The young man looked to be around seventeen or eighteen.

"Aww Aunt Char, I want two Super size Big Mac meals. I have been soooo good and I'm really hungry," he whined, turning large, pleading gray eyes to his aunt.

"No, Michael, you know what your Mom would say. Sam would kill me if she knew I let you talk me into more fast food. You're doing so well on your diet and, for a short woman, your Mom has quite a temper."

"Yep," the young man replied with pride. "But she never stays mad for long," he finished with a grin.

His Aunt Char seemed to be considering this comment for a moment when a loud noise in the rear of the restaurant drew everyone's attention. First there was yelling, then screams closely followed by gunshots.

Dylan reacted instantly. Drawing Lura to her and shielding the smaller woman with her own body, she threw them both to the floor. Lura felt the tall soldier stiffen just before she was folded into two strong arms.

"Dylan, what's going on? What happened?"

Dylan immediately recognized the sound of the gunshots. Her first thoughts were to get Lura to safety. Suddenly she was back in the cave facing the big gun of the tank. Dylan's vision tunneled until all she saw was the threat.

As Lura watched, Dylan changed. Gone was the smiling soldier. Gone was the gentle, sweet lover. The person rising to stand over her was dangerously familiar. The face was a chiseled mask and the eyes were an icy blue.

The Hawk had returned. She stood and silently walked out to face the thief.

The commotion and the gunshots were caused by, a slender young man with dirty blonde hair, who stood boldly in the back of the restaurant. He was dressed in a dark green jacket two sizes too big, black gloves that could not hide his slender hands and a blue baseball cap turned with the bill in back.

Jarrod had been in this McDonald's before and had his routine down pat. Like his mind, his n plan was simple. He would wave his gun around, fire off a few rounds, threaten a few faint-hearted customers and employees and rob the popular eatery. It had always worked before and he needed a few bucks for the new speakers he was wanted to go with the sound system he had stolen last night. Yep, he would impress the girls when he rolled out in his low rider with the new boomers. His mind had already installed the speakers and he was rolling down the streets in his dreams, leaning back in the seat, the windows down and the paint vibrating off the car.

When he arrived in the restaurant he expected some resistance, but he had not counted on the creature he now faced. Before him was a demon with a woman's face. The lips were drawn back exposing white teeth in a chilling grin. Her mane of hair seemed to dance, alive around her shoulders, but it was the eyes that were the most frightening of all. The irises were almost white and as cold as death.

Lura watched as the would-be thief froze in place. His hands trembled as he stared into the face of the very tall, very angry soldier. He stood still, not moving a muscle, the way one would if facing a rabid wolf.

Lura watched in utter amazement as he stopped in his tracks with arms outstretched, palms down. His eyes still locked with Dylan's, he slowly bent and lowered his weapon to the floor, then stood, waiting. Dylan had not moved. She had not spoken or threatened him in any way. Dylan Hawke had simply glared at the trembling man while he, to his total embarrassment, wet his pants in sheer terror.

A quick thinking employee had picked up a phone in the manager's office and dialed 911. The sound of the siren and the arrival of the police brought a cheer from the crowd, but there was nothing from the still figure of the soldier or trembling form of the thief.

The police special operations unit rushed the restaurant, guns drawn, expecting to find cowering customers. Instead, they too faced a very angry Captain Hawke. Lura knew that Dylan was not herself. She had tried to stop the police from further escalating the situation, but it was too late and they moved too quickly.

Rushing towards the tall woman the SWAT team attempted to reach for the arms of the two people facing each other so threateningly. Dylan felt them coming and she spun around ready to face the newest threat. Crouching low, she now placed herself firmly between the guns and Lura.

"Put your hands up, Miss!" a stunned young police officer ordered, training his weapon on the angry dark haired woman.

"No!" Lura screamed, rushing forward. She dodged around Dylan and, standing with her back to the policeman, spoke in a soft voice.

"It's alright, Sweetheart. These are the good guys. These are the cops. Everything is okay now. Calm down, we're okay."

From what seemed like a great distance, Dylan heard Lura's voice. Struggling in a daze, she began to focus on the soft green eyes. Shaking her head she began to listen to the voice of her soulmate.

"Everything is okay, these are the police," Lura

repeated. Slowly, Dylan realized that the threat was gone. She was no longer in the desert, and most importantly, Lura was safe. Reaching out like a blind woman searching through the dark, she folded the smaller woman to her chest, breathing in the smell of familiar shampoo.

The same perky reporter and cameramen rushed forward shoving the cameras and mike into the soldier's face. She stepped back when the mike picked up a low rumbling growl. She frowned, tapped the mike to check the sound level then, undaunted, pointed it again towards the couple.

"Can you tell us what just happened here, Ms. Hawke? How do you feel right now, having just stopped a hold up"?

This time it was the blonde who answered; she had had enough. Lura turned from Dylan to face the reporter, pushing her back and glared into the camera until the cameraman finally caught a hint and lowered the thing. Sparks seemed to fly from the green eyes of the small woman. She suddenly seemed very, very intimidating. He had thought at first that the tall dark woman was the one to watch out for, but now he was not so sure. He looked first at the little blond then the quiet dark haired woman.

Dylan stood there her eyes tightly closed, arms wrapped around herself, in a state of shock.

The manager of the McDonald's stepped in front of the camera; he had already talked to the stunned law enforcement officers about the dark woman. He told them how she had subdued the thief before they arrived. He was attempting to explain what they all had seen, but could not believe: a woman stopping a robbery with a glare.

As the police cuffed the thief, the manager finished his conversation with the camera and slowly approached the two women. "Thank you for stopping that asshole. That is the third time in two months that he's been in here. The police have never been able to catch him. Somehow, I don't think he will be coming back this time," he said, smiling. "Now I know you weren't here for the 'entertainment', so whatever it is you wanted, it's on the house."

Lura smiled and thanked the manager. She started to turn the offer down when she heard a deep voice respond, "French fries, and a Dr. Pepper."

Lura turned and glanced back at her partner. Dylan still had the disturbed look in her eyes, but if she wanted French fries, by God, she was going to get them.

"Super-size that and add a Strawberry shake to it."

"I'll do better than that." He walked to the counter and pulled out a slip of paper. He quickly wrote out a note and signed it, then passed it to Lura, still staring at her dark friend.

The note read: **"Free French fries, Dr. Pepper and Strawberry shake for life at this McDonalds."** It was signed: **"John Wilson, owner/manager."** Lura chuckled and passed the note to Dylan, who glanced at it briefly before stuffing it into the pocket of her jeans and turning an expectant glare at the manager.

John Wilson had not flipped a burger or salted a fry in years, but he jumped to fill this order. Pushing aside the startled teenager behind the deep fryer, he shook out the fry basket and dumped the hot fries into the bin.

"She likes lots of salt," Lura added, trying to keep the smile out of her voice. Turning again to face her lover, Lura took Dylan's hand and led her back to their seats past the looks of gratitude on the faces of the other patrons.

Dylan sat with her back to a wall, her eyes scanning the open spaces between their seat and the door. Waiting. Lura watched as Dylan pulled a napkin from the dispenser on the table and slowly tore it in half then half again and again until there was nothing but a small pile of white confetti.

"Getting ready for a parade love?" Lura asked.

"Huh, what? Oh, sorry sweetheart. What did you say?" Dylan asked, focusing worried eyes on her companion.

"I asked if you were getting ready for a ticker tape?" Lura asked smiling.

"No, sorry. I guess I am a bit distracted," the dark woman said. "That guy just shook me up a bit. I kinda forgot where I was for a minute there," Dylan said as she stared at the small pile of snowy napkin bits. She gently gathered the pieces and placed them in the brass colored ashtray at the next table.

Turning to Dylan, Lura noticed the worried frown on her face and reached up to stroke the dark hair from her lover's eyes. "Honey, what's wrong? Is what happened still getting to you? I know that things moved pretty quickly, but it's over now so lets just enjoy our snack and go back to the hotel. I know it has been a long month, but we can go home after this."

"Home?" Dylan asked just as John brought over a tray loaded with fresh hot fries and two large drink cups. Lura was sure she had heard Dylan mumble something, but wasn't sure what it was.

I need to get her back to the hotel so we can get into some soft clothes and do some serious cuddling, I

24

think my big bad warrior could use a bit of snuggle time she thought, watching the still frowning woman munch on the hot fries and glare at the door.

CHAPTER 3

The walk back to the hotel was thankfully uneventful. Lura spent the majority of it trying to revive the atmosphere and by the time they turned up the drive she had succeeded in getting Dylan to unwind enough to allow the circulation to return to the hand gripping hers. The ride up in the elevator resulted in a poking tickle fight and by the time they had reached their room, Dylan's good humor was on an upswing.

Lura knew what would keep that happy mood. She reached for her toiletry bag and walked into the bathroom. Turning on the hot tap she squirted a generous amount of scented oil into the running water. Adding a touch of cold she filled the tub as the crisp sent of evergreens filled the air. Satisfied that the water wasn't too hot she turned and called out, "Dylan honey, take off your clothes!"

A laughing disembodied voice replied, "Lura, I know I usually take charge in the bedroom, and I know I promised that you could be in charge sometimes, but Sweetie you are going a bit overboard don't ya think?"

"Dylan!" Lura laughed, coming out of the bathroom holding a large towel while advancing on her lover with a look of determination on her face.

"Now you listen to me, Hawke. If you are not naked in the next fifteen seconds you are gonna see one very pissed off little falcon. You hear me?" Lura stood there, her hands on her hips and watched as a grinning Dylan stripped. As she turned to place her clothes on the bed Dylan felt the towel smack her naked butt.

"HEY!" she yelped turning to face a smiling pair of green eyes.

"Get that cute butt of yours in the tub, Hawke, before the water gets cold," Lura laughed.

"Alright, alright, just keep your flippin' towel to yourself," Dylan said as she ran bouncing into the bathroom and stepped into the tub. "Ya gonna join me? It looks big enough for two."

"Nope, not this time, lover. This one is all yours; you earned it. But hey, if you ask really nice, I might be persuaded to scrub your back," Lura replied

Dylan sank into the hot, scented water of the tub and allowed the soft oily water to caress her body. "Lura, this is great. All I need is a..."

"Dr Pepper?" Lura said, appearing in the doorway with a sweating can of cold Dr. Pepper.

"God, I love this woman," Dylan said as she reached for the can.

Lura smiled as she watched the exhausted woman sip on the cold soda, a crooked grin on her lips. Her eyes traveled the length of the beautiful bronzed body peeking through the steam, frowning as they touched on the still healing scars made by the bullets. Her Hawk had been through Hell. The question wasn't if she survived, but did her soul make it as well?

Dylan lay back with a deep sigh, relaxing and finally feeling a measure of security behind the locked door of the hotel room. Her soulmate was here and safe, she was here and safe. The doors were locked and she was on the fourth floor, in her own room and in her own country. There was no need to worry, no worries, no worries…

As Lura watched as Dylan closed her eyes and slipped deeper into the tub. At first she was worried that the sleeping woman would slip under the water but her long legs prevented that from happening. Lura decided to let her relax. "This is probably the first decent rest she has had in days," Lura thought. Turning, she headed back to the bedroom. "I'll give her a few minutes, but I swear if she comes out of there looking like a prune…"

Dylan felt the sweat dripping down her face; she was hot and it was nighttime. He was coming, no not for her, for Lura. He was going to hurt Lura! *I have to get to her before he does!* The sand was so thick, she was sinking into it. *Quicksand! I can't run! Have to get to Lura! She is in the cave surrounded by my men. They can't fight him, they have no arms, no legs, no heads. They can't protect her. She will die, like they did. I have to get to her! Lura!*

"LURA!" Dylan screamed, leaping from the tub, sliding on the now wet floor and crashing to her knees.

"Lura!" she cried, fear in her voice. Lura heard her from the bedroom and rushed in to find a sodden Dylan on her hands and knees beside the tub. Her face was streaked with tears and her hair was in disarray.

"Dylan honey, are you okay?" She bent to help the tall woman to her feet. Reaching for a towel to wrap around the wet body she guided the still stunned soldier into the bedroom and onto the bed. She ran back into the bathroom and returned moments later with two towels. She wrapped one around Dylan's shaking shoulders and she knelt in front of the soldier and with the other towel, began drying her shaking legs, rubbing briskly to warm her blood.

A stunned Dylan watched her soulmate. Drawn by the need to reassure herself of Lura's presence, she reached up with an unsteady hand to stroke the creamy cheek. "So soft." She glanced into gentle green eyes. Placing her hand behind Lura's head she slowly drew the soft pink lips to her own, kissing the blonde gently. She released Lura from the kiss, her hands pulling the shirt from Lura's waist.

Lura threw her head back offering her lover a choice bit of neck to nuzzle and moaned softly as Dylan took advantage of the opportunity. Her lips brushed a pale throat, pausing to enjoy the throbbing of a quickening pulse. Her tongue gently reached out to touch warm flesh and she was pleased to feel the pulse become more rapid. Slowly her hands reached around Lura's trembling body, her palm slipping up and around an expanding ribcage, lifting a soft shirt over blonde hair.

"I love you, Lura." Dylan pulled Lura to her and began to undress the other woman, kissing each portion of flesh as it was exposed.

Lura felt the chilled air touch her skin, her flesh trembled with anticipation and she felt Dylan slip her hands around her back and release the catch on her bra. Warm hands slipped up and gently stroked her breasts and she felt her stomach knot with anticipation. The hands moved up under her arms and lifted her up and forward. Lura opened her eyes and stared into the deep blue crystals of Dylan's eyes. She saw the pain and love reflected there. She reached out and pulled the towel from around the trembling shoulders, her eyes never leaving Dylan's. Slowly her fingers traced trembling lips. She slipped one inside and watched as the blue eyes closed and the lips closed around her finger. A warm tongue stroked the soft pad of her fingertip.

Dylan's hands slid back down Lura's body, and slipped into the waist of the soft denim jeans. Buttons released their hold on the pants and they slipped down slender legs. Panties quickly followed jeans and Lura now stood naked and exposed in front of her lover.

Dylan rested her hands on Lura's hips as she gently pushed her back and let her eyes roam every inch of the beautiful body. Lura waited patiently, her eyes heavy lidded as she watched Dylan examine her. The blue eyes roamed her body, stopping at the now glistening mass of golden hair at her groin. The tip of a pink tongue emerged from Dylan's mouth as she licked suddenly parched lips. Her eyes continued on their journey, stopping again at exposed breasts, the pink nipples now erect and tempting.

Slowly she pulled Lura back towards her as she slid to edge of the bed. Watching the blonde's face she slipped her knees between Lura's legs. Spreading her legs she forced Lura to a sitting position. Her legs wide and her thighs resting on Dylan's, Lura could feel the cool air caressing her wet groin as hands now reached back to cup her ass.

Bending slowly, Dylan drew an erect nipple into her mouth. She sucked gently as she massaged the soft skin under her hands. Lura buried her hands in Dylan's hair and held on for dear life. She felt one hand move up towards her waist but paused only to continue around her thigh, the fingers tickling the curls that covered her now aching clit. Slowly, gently the fingers parted her and slipped inside.

Dylan felt the wetness on her fingertips and groaned in pleasure. She pressed two fingers around a hardening clit and gently squeezed. Lura groaned in ecstasy and tightened her thighs, lifting her body to meet the searching fingers.

Dylan stroked two wet slick fingers deep inside Lura, stroking her clit with a thumb as she slowly pumped in and out. She could feel the muscles inside her lover tighten around her fingers; Lura was close to the edge. She slowed and pulled out, smiling when she heard the groan of disappointment. She leaned back releasing the tortured nipple and staring into hot hungry green eyes. She lowered her gaze to the neglected nipple and brought her hand up to carefully paint the pink flesh with the wetness clinging to her fingers. Sure that every bit of the nipple was covered, she watched Lura's face as she brought the fingers to her lips and slowly licked them clean while closing her eyes and groaning out her enjoyment.

Lura felt the wetness flowing again from her body as Dylan now locked her lips around the glistening nipple and sucked gently. She turned on the bed and lowered Lura to the mattress. With one last tug on the aching nipple she released it, only to let her tongue train down her lover's body to bury itself deep in the blond curls. She licked the hard clit she found there. Lifting her head she stared deep into green eyes as she reached down and captured Lura's thighs, spreading her legs wide. Dylan knelt before her lover and buried her face in the sweet wet moistness she found there.

She pushed Lura back onto the bed and forced her legs further apart. Lying between them, she relaxed to enjoy her meal.

Lura felt as if her body would explode as Dylan sucked and nibbled on her clit. Her hips thrust upward in an effort to offer more of herself to her hungry mate. Finally, with a deep guttural moan, she came. Her body trembled with an exquisite orgasm, her hands buried in the glossy black mane. Exhausted, she watched, fascinated as Dylan licked her thighs clean of every glistening drop she could find and then smiled up at her.

Lura smiled back. "My turn, Hawk," she purred.

CHAPTER 4

Later that evening, Dylan lay awake, the hum of the room's air conditioning the only sound she heard. Her left arm pillowed her head; her right was wrapped around the smaller woman that clung to her side like a limpet. All should have been right with her world; she was home, safe, warm, fed and deeply in love. She could not understand why she lay there staring at the ceiling. Her mind was alive and refused to allow her eyes to close. Every time she felt herself drift off, visions would appear in her head. Visions of her men, of the tank, of the men she had killed, and of her soulmate, beaten and bloody. She knew the visions were all in the past, but she could not seem to convince her mind to leave them there. The incident earlier in the day simply triggered the memories again and this frightened her. She was afraid of her response; she had lost control. What could have happened if Lura had not been there, what would she have done to the cops, to those people in the McDonald's, hell even to the thief?

I have to control this. I can't let it control me. Dylan lay there staring at the ceiling, seeing the incident repeat itself over and over again. That was

33

how Lura found her the next morning, still staring at the ceiling, dark circles under her exhausted, dull blue eyes.

"Dylan honey, you didn't get any sleep last night. Why don't you lay here and let me get us some breakfast? Then I want you to go back to bed and stay there," Lura said

Dylan looked up from her place on the bed staring into the eyes of her soulmate. At first she was a bit upset, not liking the idea of being coddled, but then she realized what Lura had said.

"I will make a deal with you sweetheart. I will stay in bed if I am not alone," Dylan said, wiggling her eyebrows and giving Lura a decidedly wicked grin.

The small blonde grinned back thinking that Dylan must not be too tired if she was having those kinds of thoughts. *Yipee!* "I'll be right back," she said. Grabbing her robe she ran from the room to the laughter of her roommate.

As soon as Lura left the room Dylan began to remember again the horror of the dream. As she lay there her mind began to run through the events of the previous day again. *What if I had hurt someone? What if Lura had been hurt? What could have happened to those people in the McDonald's? I could have really caused some damage. My God I could have hurt someone.* Dylan was so lost in thought that she did not hear the door open or Lura call out. Suddenly, she was just there.

"Dylan honey, I have the…"

Dylan jumped and swung a fist towards the intrusion. She tried to stop herself, but she was too late. The tray held by the smaller woman went flying, the hot coffee spilled down the blonde's chest and she screamed, slapping at her robe. Dylan sprang from the bed, grabbed the linen sheets and dabbed at the brown liquid running down the front of the robe.

"Lura! Baby, I am so sorry. Are you okay? Please, I am so sorry, tell me if you are burned anywhere. I am so sorry. Please, Lura."

"Calm down Dylan, I'm fine. It didn't get me; the robe got most of it. I'm okay, really. You didn't hurt me. I should know better than to slip up on a soldier without any forewarning. I am really sorry I startled you." Lura gently sat on the edge of the bed taking Dylan's hand in hers, feeling it tremble from the recent shock. Her heart went out to the stunned woman and she gathered her close, rubbing her back gently to calm her.

Dylan could not believe her reaction, it was everything that she had imagined in her nightmares. The only difference is that it had happened to the one person that she would give her life to protect. She sighed deeply and buried her face in her hands.

Oh God, what is going on? I nearly hurt Lura. I have to get control of this thing.

Lura sat, watching the woman she loved, feeling the intense pain she was suffering but having no idea how to help. So she sat quietly rubbing Dylan's back and offering her silent support.

Finally Dylan straightened and turned to Lura. "Can we get out of here for a bit? I need a break. I need some air. Maybe it will help me get my head together."

"Sure sweetheart, let's get dressed and go for a walk. How does that sound? Hey maybe we can stop at that McDonalds and try a breakfast, okay?"

"No, not the McDonalds, I…I….I'm not hungry."

Dylan never was a good liar and this lie was as clear as glass. Lura looked at the worried expression on Dylan's face and realize the problem. "Okay honey, no problem. Maybe you will be hungry after our walk," she said, rubbing Dylan's back in a soothing circular motion. "Tell ya what, there's a bagel shop right down the road near a park. We can walk there, pick up some breakfast and eat in the park. Maybe we will be hungry by the time we get there. How does that sound?"

"Great, that sounds great, Lura. Yeah, let's get dressed and go."

Suddenly she couldn't get out of the confines of her sanctuary fast enough. Dylan sprang naked from the bed and moved to the dresser. Finding and slipping into a clean bra and panties, she reached in again and pulled out a pair of black jeans and a sleeveless white polo shirt. She quickly slipped them on then, reaching back into the dresser, she located a pair of clean socks and crawled under the bed for her Nike's. Finally dressed she stood by the door waiting, not so patiently, for her partner.

Lura had been watching this entire exercise with amazement. She knew how fast Dylan could undress but she had just set a new land speed record for dressing. Shaking her head she finished tying her own shoes and stood, smoothing down the front of her green polo shirt and tucking the tail into the dark blue jeans she had chosen to wear.

Leaving the room the two quickly walked down the hall and into the next elevator. A smooth silent ride down took them to the lobby where they checked for messages and left their key cards. Since they were walking they didn't want to risk losing them. They walked side by side through the busy town, past the McDonald's that was in the midst of the breakfast rush, and on towards the park. Lura was nearly trotting to keep up with her partner's long legged stride.

"Dylan, Dylan honey, please slow down," Lura panted. "My legs aren't nearly as long as yours and I never was real good in track events."

"Huh? What was that...?" Dylan was distracted, her mind a hundred miles away. All she could think of was the forest.

Lura reached out a hand and grabbed Dylan's arm. "Please Dylan, slow down. I'm out of breath." Dylan stopped when she felt the tug on her arm. Glancing down she realized that Lura wasn't at her side. She stood for a second a bit disoriented then, as if realizing something odd, she turned and saw her blond companion several feet away. Lura had stopped and placing her hands on her hips had tilted her head back and was sucking in large lungs full of air.

Seeing the obvious distress she had caused her mate Dylan looked down at her shoes in embarrassment. "Um, sorry Lura, I guess I was a bit distracted with the idea of getting out," she stuttered. "Are you okay? I'll slow down, promise."

Lura waited catching her breath before she answered. Walking up to Dylan she placed a hand on her shoulder and smiled. "Hey, I understand, you have been cooped up so long I'm surprised you didn't bolt sooner. Come on, let's get to the park and then I can take a real break." She slid her arm through Dylan's and turned them both in the direction on the park.

"Wow, do you smell that?" Lura asked Dylan.

Frowning, the taller woman paused and tilted her head, closing her eyes to concentrate.

"Oh yeah, cinnamon and walnut, with just a touch of honey," she commented.

"How does she do that?" Lura asked, no one in particular. Dylan smiled overhearing the comment.

They reached the bakery where Dylan held the door and with a bow and a wave, allowed Lura to enter first. Smiling at the wonderful warm smell of freshly baking bread, Lura walked up to the counter and began examining the selection. There was quite a bit to choose from. Cinnamon raisin, honey and walnut, whole wheat, blueberry and the choices went on. Dylan stood back with a smile on her face as her partner selected first one then another, changing her mind at least three times before settling on the blueberry with strawberry cream cheese already on it. Dylan selected the cinnamon raisin with honey walnut cream cheese in a separate plastic container. Smiling, she paid for the bagels and took the brown bag from the extremely patient waitress and handed it to Lura as they left the bakery.

"Honey?" Lura asked the silent smiling woman pacing next to her. "Um, why did you insist on your cream cheese be put in a separate container instead of on your bagel?"

"Well, the true 'bagel connoisseur' knows that the only way to correctly eat a bagel is with the cream cheese slathered on all available surfaces," Dylan informed the curious blond.

"Slather? Is that really a word?" Lura asked, trying in vain to keep the smile out of her voice.

"Of course it is." the tall woman replied with

confidence, "I just used it in a perfectly good sentence, didn't I? The only way to truly slather is if you have plenty of cream cheese. Thus the need for the separate container."

She wrapped her arm over the blonde's shoulder and gave her a friendly hug as they continued on towards the park.

It took Dylan a good fifteen minutes of dedicated evaluation to decide on the perfect location to enjoy their meal. Lura was at the end of her patience and ready to find any handy spot of shade when the tall soldier finally settled on "the perfect spot" near the edge of a large field beneath the arms of several huge ancient oaks. Dylan explained in some detail how the only avenue of approach to their location was straight on and that she could handle any flanking maneuvers because she would have plenty of time to prepare. Lura simply smiled indulgently and nodded her agreement even if she didn't understand half of what she had just been told. If Dylan was happy, she was happy.

The two women found a shady spot under one of the huge old oaks and settled down to have their breakfast. Part way through they began to watch the young people playing Frisbee football on the field in front of them. Lura was amused at the intensity of her companion's viewing, Dylan sat yelling out encouragement to the young would-be athletes and laughingly cursing at their sometimes clumsy efforts. All in all it had turned into a wonderful morning.

Having finished her bagel, Dylan stood and shook the crumbs out of her shirt. "Lura, I'm going over to the rest room and clean the cream cheese off my face. Slathering tends to be a bit messy." The dark haired woman smiled down at her companion, bits of bagel and cream cheese still evident on her lips.

"Bend down a minute, honey," Lura called reaching for the slender bronzed hand. She pulled Dylan down to her and gently but thoroughly cleaned the cream cheese from her mouth, much to the happy chagrin of the soldier. "Um, just couldn't let you walk around with slathering on your face, darlin', " Lura commented with a heavy, sexy southern drawl.

"Oh, well, we can't have that now can we?" the laughing woman commented. She smiled down at her companion then with a quick kiss, turned and strode off towards the restrooms. Lura watched the tall slender woman, admiring the gentle sway of her hips and the rolling gate of her long legs. Momentarily distracted, she did not notice the Frisbee game coming closer and closer. As she watched and waited for Dylan's return her mind had drifted back to the oasis in the desert and that wonderful afternoon bath they had shared. She still remembered the tall beautiful soldier standing naked in the sun, the light glittering off the drops of water sliding down the beautiful bronzed body. With that thought in mind and a dreamy look on her face she continued to stare in the direction her love had gone and missed the young man running straight at her.

Dylan had just finished cursing at the hand blow dryers and had left the rest room when a sudden movement caught her eye. Her head jerked up as she saw a man struggling with her partner. All sound stopped as she heard Lura scream. She didn't remember running, she just remembered suddenly being there. She reached down and pulled the man off of Lura and threw him against a tree, her strong hands locking onto his shirt collar and holding him off the ground, his feet dangling.

"You will not touch her!"

"Dylan!" Lura screamed, "Let him go, it was just an accident. Let him go." Lura reached out her hand and rested it on a tense arm, the corded muscles straining in the effort to hold the man against the tree. "Please, honey, put him down." The voice was calm and broke through the red haze in her mind. "Please, Dylan, please."

Lura watched the face of her lover change from anger to realization to shock as her words registered. Dylan finally realized exactly what she was doing. She lowered the young man gently to his feet, releasing his shirt and staring as he scampered off looking back over his shoulder as he reached his concerned friends.

"Boy that is one crazy, strong ass bitch," he said, brushing off his shirt. Now, in the midst of his cronies, he felt his heart rate slow to a normal rhythm and was a bit embarrassed at his behavior and fear. His friends gathered around him, patting his back and agreeing with him in an attempt to reassure themselves that he had indeed survived a meeting with a most dangerous adversary.

Dylan stood facing the tree, gazing down at her hands, the same hands that had swung at Lura, the same hands that had almost killed a thief, the same hands that almost harmed an innocent young man and the same hands that had taken so many lives. All she saw was blood.

Lura watched as Dylan froze in place her hands held palm up in front of her. Something was not right, she did not know how to help but she wanted to desperately. She couldn't stand to see the lost and hurt look in the face of the woman she loved. Reaching out slowly she placed her smaller hands in the long, slender powerful ones of the soldier and squeezed. "Let's get out of here, honey. Let's go for a drive. Better yet, let's go home."

"Home?" Dylan looked into the worried green eyes and thought of the word. "Yes, home," she said with a sad smile. She took Lura's hand and led the way back to the hotel to pack.

By the time they reached the hotel, Lura was exhausted. The stress of the morning had taken a lot of her scanty energy and she knew that she needed to rest. "Dylan, honey, can we leave in the morning? I am really worn out and I want to help you drive. If we stay tonight, we can leave first thing in the morning and avoid most of the early morning work traffic."

Dylan, still in a daze, nodded her head in agreement and went to sit on the bed. Lura watched her mate, concerned at the quiet, forlorn attitude in the usually active woman. She was worried and hoped that returning home would eliminate some of the stress Dylan was under and allow her body and mind to heal.

She went to the dresser and removed the two sleeping shirts they habitually wore, handing the soft worn gray Army shirt to Dylan. Slipping out of her own clothes she nestled into the soft Tigger shirt that she loved. It was very early, but she figured that they would probably not be going out again today so getting comfortable and relaxing was the only other option.

Having changed, she turned to see Dylan still sitting on the edge of the bed, the shirt held forgotten in her hands. "Honey, why don't you change? I'll see what's on television and we can relax on the bed. How does that sound?"

"What? What did you say Lura?" Dylan looked up confused.

"I said, why don't you change and we can get comfortable and watch television."

"Oh, yeah, sure, that's fine. I'll just change and we can get comfortable and watch a little TV, okay?"

"Um, sure Dylan, a little TV sounds good," the confused blonde said.

Dylan slipped out of her clothes and into her sleeping shirt. She pulled the covers back and slid in between the cool sheets. Holding her arms wide, she invited Lura to snuggle. Lura couldn't seem to move fast enough to crawl onto the bed and into the strong waiting arms. Snuggling down into the warm embrace she sighed contentedly and smiled as Dylan reached for the remote and adjusted the picture.

Things are almost back to normal she thought. *I am not sure what is going on in that beautiful dark head of yours but I need to get you somewhere you can think, my big bad warrior* Lura thought, gazing up through sleepy lashes at her companion.

Dylan lay in bed in the dark, the only light coming from the television that was now showing a rerun of a Conan Doyle show. Her mind was a million miles away. She lay staring at the silent figures, she had turned down the sounds so as not to wake her bedmate. Though she was watching the host go through the motions of the interview, her eyes were seeing the scenes that had taken place over three yeas ago. Silent tears glistened on her cheeks and she made no effort to wipe them away as she was almost unaware of them.

I have got to get a grip. This flying off the handle is really going to cause some serious problems. I just don't know what to do and how to handle it. I can't stay around, Lura; look what has already happened. She glanced down at the sleeping woman and pulled her closer, placing a kiss on her blond head. *I know who can help me. I just have to get to him. I have to find him. Sorry, I can't take you with me, Little Falcon, but I will be back, or at least I will try to come back. I just can't stay around you any longer. I won't take the chance of hurting you.*

Silently, Dylan slipped her arms out from under the mumbling woman and slid out of bed. She quickly dressed and packed her bag. She turned to walk out and then gazed one last time at the beautiful sleeping woman. *I can't just leave. I'll leave her a note so she won't worry.*

Sitting at the small desk in the room she opened the drawer and pulled out a pen and the hotel note pad.

Little Falcon,

I am not sure what is going on in my head, but I can't take the chance of hurting you or causing you any pain. My nightmares are becoming impossible to distinguish from reality. I need to go somewhere where I can't hurt anyone, especially you.

Know that I love you and I will until the day I die.
Your Hawk,
Dylan

She placed a soft kiss at the bottom to seal the note then placed it on the pillow her head had been resting on scant minutes before. Reaching out with a long slender hand she caressed the soft cheek, her eyes tearing at the smile she received from the gesture. Then, quickly, before she changed her mind, she turned and walked silently out the door and out of Lura's life.

CHAPTER 5

Lura felt the cold air hit her skin. She had kicked the sheet off in her sleep and the air conditioning was working overtime. She was surprised that Dylan had not replaced the covers.

"Dylan? Dylan honey, its cold. Come back to bed and let's snuggle," Lura called, her eyes still closed.

No response.

"Dylan? Dylan where are you?" Lura opened one sleepy green eye and scanned the empty room. Climbing from the bed she staggered to the bathroom and peeked inside.

"Dylan are you in here?" *That was a dumb question* she thought glancing around. *Now where did that woman of mine get to?*

"Dylan, Dy…" she paused spotting the note on the cold pillow. Picking it up she quickly read through it.

"Oh my God. No. DYLAN?!" Running to the door she jerked it open startling the maid cleaning the room across the hall.

"Um, sorry, have you seen a tall dark haired woman leave this room?" The maid smiled and glanced at Lura's sleep shirt.

"Uh, no ma'am, I haven't. You might try the desk, but I would put on some clothes first if I were you."

Blushing Lura thanked the maid then went back to her room. Sitting on the bed she picked up the note and read it again slowly, her fingers brushing the soft lip prints left by her Hawk.

Where have you gone? How will I find you? Don't you know I can't live without you? Teardrops struck the paper, blurring the ink and causing Lura to cry even harder. Suddenly, the phone rang, startling her from her thoughts.

"Yes? DYLAN?" she asked

"No dear, it's your mother," came a cheery Southern voice on the other end. I just finished reading the article about you in the paper. We are proud of you dear, being nominated for that nice little writer's award, but enough of this nonsense now Lura. Your father and I have been waiting for you to come home. When might that be, dear? I need to plan a proper homecoming celebration. Your sister is here visiting and we just can't wait to see you," the voice on the other end of the line exclaimed.

"Mother? How... when...what?"

"Well dear we have now covered the four critical issues, haven't we? When are you coming home, sugar?"

"Today mother, I am coming home today," Lura said dejectedly, crumbling the note in her trembling hand. If Dylan didn't want her anymore then so be it. She told her mother that she had to make some arrangements, but she would call later with the plane departure and arrival information.

47

"Wonderful dear, your father and I will be there to meet you. You be careful now. You don't know what sort of strange people you might meet in those public waiting areas." With that remark, the phone went dead.

Lura stood there for a few minutes staring at the receiver, unsure of what to do next. Then she felt the paper in her balled up fist. Lifting her hand she started to throw the hated piece of paper into the trash bin, but could not bring herself to open her hand and release it. Slowly she sat back down on the bed and carefully flattened out the wad. She read the short note again and again, but the words didn't change. Dylan had left her.

Finally she pulled herself together. *Home, I have to go home. I can think there.*

Now, having made the decision, she couldn't move fast enough. Kneeling on the floor, she opened her suitcase and noticed the single set of toilet articles where there had earlier been two. They had just repacked everything yesterday with the idea of leaving today. Well, the plan really had not changed only instead of an 'us' decision it had been a 'me' decision. In a slight daze, Lura removed a pair of soft jeans, some under things and a pale yellow polo shirt. Slipping out of her nightshirt she quickly tossed it into the bag and pulled on her street clothes. Glancing around, she looked for her Dockers. Finally rooting though her bag again she found them in the bottom of the suitcase. Holding them she sat on the bed and reached for the phone, dialing a number from memory.

"Reservations, please." She wiggled into her shoes into her shoes while she waited to be connected. "Yes, I need a ticket to Richmond, Virginia, one way."

Dylan stared out the window of the bus as the road signs whipped by. All she could think of was Lura. Was she awake yet? Was she all right? Her heart skipped as she thought of the events of the last few days.

I'm doing the right thing, I know I am. So why do I feel like shit? She listened to the hum of the tires and the muted music coming from her seatmate's headset. The young man sitting next to her was in uniform, a brand new soldier. She sighed and wondered if he really knew what it was all about. Glancing at him out of the corner of her eye she noted the crossed rifles of the infantry insignia on his lapel and smiled. *A grunt.* He had his rifleman badge proudly displayed shining on his left breast pocket right below his Army service ribbon. *The walkin' and breathin' ribbon. Probably just finished boot camp and heading home to his girl,* Dylan thought, smiling sadly.

Looking at this young boy soldier with his short cut hair and his freshly shaved face brought back memories of another young man, a young officer who had just begun to live, a California boy who died before he reached his 23rd birthday. Dylan closed her eyes, seeing the fresh suntanned face again, the strawberry blond hair and the contagious smile.

"Um, are you alright, ma'am?" A voice startled her from her memories. She opened her eyes and realized that the young soldier was speaking to her.

"I just... well, I kinda saw you were crying. Is there someone bothering you? Is there something I can do?" He held out a clean handkerchief, the sound of genuine concern in his voice.

Dylan stared at the small white cloth, and was startled to realize that she was crying. "No, but thanks for the offer and the hanky," she said, taking the cloth and wiping her face.

"No problem ma'am, you keep that," he said, pushing the handkerchief back at her. "I will be close by if you need some help. Okay?" He offered, puffing out his narrow chest with confidence.

Dylan smiled remembering all the young men she had killed over the last three years. *I wonder if any of them had girls back home waiting for them?* Outwardly she thanked the young soldier again and turned back to the window to continue her silent vigil. Watching the landscape change like the setting sun, from the congested traffic and tall buildings of the city to the open freedom and evergreen scent of the country. She was going home.

The droning of the tires seemed to be chanting, 'Going home, going home, going home." The clean scent of pine even overrode the faint smell of the diesel fuel floating around the bus. Finally, with her head resting against the cool pane of the window and the hum of the tires rumbling in her ears, she nodded off.

At that same moment, Lura's flight was taking off for Richmond. The pull of the plane's powerful engines reminded her of another flight, one much longer and into the unknown. The end of that flight had led her into life threatening danger and the death of friends. While those thoughts were painful on bright memory shown through it all. That flight had also led her to the woman she loved. The one person she believed to be the other half of her soul. Now she was on another plane, and this trip was very different. She knew exactly where she was going. There was no threat at the end of it and the only death she would face was the death of her heart. She could not understand how a heart torn in so many pieces could continue to beat. She sat, going over the last few days in her head. Her mind was so distracted she wasn't sure what day it was much less aware of the fact that the plane had landed and all the other passengers had already left.

A voice broke into her thoughts and she looked up to see a smiling stewardess calling her. "Miss, we have landed. Are you alright, do you need some help?" The concern in the woman's voice made Lura aware of the tears streaming down her face.

"No, no, I'm fine, just a bit stressed," she stated, taking an offered napkin and wiping her face. "Sorry, I didn't realize we had arrived. I'll just get my bag and be out of your way." She stood and reached into the overhead compartment and pulled out her small carry-on bag. Sighing deeply she shouldered the bag and made her way out of the plane.

The lobby of the airport was crowded and noisy; the airport authority had gotten the passengers into long lines to clear airport security. She moved into one of them and while she waited patiently for her bag and identification to be checked, her mind was reading the note over and over again. She still had one question, why? Why had she left? Her heart hurt with every beat and she felt so alone. There was no one waiting, no blue eyes smiling at her. She was alone.

Finally leaving the long lines behind, Lura was looking around for any familiar face when she saw a stranger holding a sign with her name on it. Thomas looked around, hoping that the person he had been sent to pick up would hurry. He had a cold dinner and a hot wife waiting at home. He noticed the small attractive young blonde approaching; she wore a pair of faded jeans and a pale yellow polo shirt. A small bag was slung over her shoulder and she pulled a larger matching bag behind her.

For someone who just got back from vacation she sure don't look happy he thought. *Well, that ain't my problem, I just got to get her home in one piece.* Aloud he said, "Ms Grant? Lura Grant?"

"Yes," came the soft reply.

"Um, your folks sent me to pick you up. I'm the new chauffer, my name is Thomas." He held out his hand for her bag and was surprised to find her hand grasping his in a firm handshake.

"Nice to meet you, Thomas. Where is the car parked?" the quiet woman asked, looking into the startled brown eyes of the young man.

He reached again for her bag, but she turned towards the street looking for the car. He was finally able to pull the larger bag from her grasp and was surprised when she didn't protest. "Right this way ma'am, I have the car parked right outside. Do you have any other bags?"

"No, I have nothing," came the soft reply.

Somehow, I don't think she is talkin' about bags the young driver surmised.

They reached the stretch Lincoln and he held the door open for the slender woman to enter. He ran to the rear and with the flick of a switch popped open the trunk and stored the larger bag in the back.

Lura sat gazing out the window as they pulled out, listening to the hum of the tires. They seemed to talk to her. "She's gone away, she's gone away, she's gone away." The tears began again.

CHAPTER 6

The bus finally stopped and Dylan woke to a scene of confusion. People were standing outside waiting to get on and people were standing in the aisles waiting to get off. She stood and grabbed her duffel from under her seat. The young soldier had disappeared, possibly leaving at an earlier stop that she had slept through. She shouldered the heavy bag, shuffled down the aisle and off of the bus. Looking around, she got her bearings and began walking. She wasn't sure how long she walked or how far, but she remembered crossing over a highway on a nearly barren overpass. It was dark and the lights of oncoming cars blinded her. She ducked her head and kept walking.

Finally, she reached Shaconage, 'the place of blue smoke' the Qualla Reservation and the Oconaluftee Village in particular. She needed her Grandfather Gray Hawk. Walking through the reservation she did not notice the new stores that had sprung up since her departure or the crowds of tourist snapping photos of young men dressed in traditional costumes. She followed a memory of a Dylan that had left that place three long years ago. She passed the carved figurehead of Sequoyah, the inventor of the Cherokee alphabet, a brave powerful man who had led his people a hundred years ago. She staggered on drawing the attention of several of the tourists who frowned at the drawn, tired figure stumbling down the street. Dylan continued on, finally stopping far out of town in a secluded glade in the back of the Oconaluftee Village. The village was a reproduction of a Cherokee village of 250 years ago and was the home of her grandfather. He lived near the village, but rarely ventured out while tourists were about. She reached the wooden door of the small lodge and knocked. To her ears the sound was deafening, echoing off the mountains and drawing the attention of all around. She hung her head in distress and waited until the door slowly opened and moccasin covered feet came into her line of vision.

"Granddaughter?" The voice was warm and strong and loving, the tears came immediately. Dylan felt her knees buckle as she slowly crumbled at her grandfather's feet. She was exhausted, heartbroken and confused. She needed the understanding arms of her grandfather.

Gray Hawk was startled at the knock on his lodge door and even more surprised to see the distraught woman nearly unconscious in his doorway. He bent to help his granddaughter to her feet and led her into the lodge. Setting her in the rocker he had just left, he hurried into the kitchen and heated some water for tea. Returning, he grabbed a blanket from the sofa and wrapped the trembling woman in it.

Dylan was in a daze; she had not eaten since the

bagels in the park almost two days previously and with the exception of the light nap on the bus had not slept in 48 hours. She was at the end of her still meager reserve.

"Grandfather? Grandfather, you have to help me. I don't know what to do. It seems like my mind is slipping, I see things that aren't there. My God I almost killed an innocent man." Dylan looked up, her eyes large and nearly black in her pale face.

"Tell me, Granddaughter, when was the last time you slept?"

"I am not sure Grandfather, one maybe two days ago. I…I am afraid to sleep. When I sleep, the visions come. They make my heart hurt from the memories."

"What is it you remember Dylan?" came the softly spoken question.

"Faces, the faces of the dead. I remember my men and I remember those men that I, that I…" Dylan hung her head, the tears spilling out onto the bright pattern of the blanket as she pulled it closer around her body. Silently the old man stood and walked to the kitchen as the kettle whistled. Dylan could hear him stirring the liquid in the tin cups he always used.

He returned from the kitchen holding two steaming cups. One he passed to Dylan, the other he placed on the table in front of him. Dylan blew gently on the hot liquid in her trembling hands, careful not to spill it. Bringing it slowly to her lips she was surprised to find it to be herb tea, bitter herb tea.

"Grandfather, what is this? It tastes awful."

"You drink that all down now, Dylan. It's good for you," he replied in a stern, no nonsense voice, his arms crossed as he stared silently down at the exhausted woman. Dylan scrunched her face at the bitter taste of the tea, but swallowed it down quickly. The heated tea landed in her stomach and burned gently, warming her from head to toe. As she lowered the cup she noticed the paper napkin with a thick BLT sandwich resting on the low table in front of her. She turned a quizzical look to her grandfather.

"I suppose you want me to do something with that, right?" He simply smiled, raised an eyebrow and waited patiently until she had finished the entire sandwich.

"Now Dylan, I want you to go upstairs and take a hot shower. You will find fresh towels and a nightshirt. It's one of mine but I figure it should fit ya."

"But Grandfather, I'm not sleepy, I need..." Dylan was halted in mid sentence by a scowling old warrior who, again, folded his arms stubbornly and simply stared at her.

"Dylan you will take your tail down that hall and shower, then if you still feel like talking, we will. You can put your bag on the bed in the spare bedroom. Go on now and quit your fussing." The old man shooed her off like an errant child. Dylan smiled indulgently then grabbed her bag and turned for the hall. Fifteen minutes and one hot shower later she returned to the spare room to put away her toiletries.

"I'll just sit here a minute and get my thoughts together." She sat on the edge of the bed and stared out into space. Five minutes later the old warrior peeked into the room to see his granddaughter sprawled out over the bed, snoring softly. The tea never let him down. Smiling gently, he lifted Dylan's legs and slipped them under the covers tucking in the edges, then finally placing a kiss on her forehead he slipped from the room turning out the light.

She had been home now for two days and she had not left her suite. Her mother was worried sick, her father had given up trying to communicate with her through the heavy door and all the servants who wanted to keep their heads on their shoulders, avoided her door like the plague. Finally, Lura decided to roll out of bed and rejoin the living. Dressing in a pair of faded jeans and a pink and white t-shirt, she slipped her feet into a pair of Nikes and headed down to the kitchen.

Lenora, the main cook, bottle washer and guardian of the kitchen and all that entailed, was busy cutting tomatoes for the lunch salad when she slipped in. Grabbing a carrot from the pile of freshly washed vegetables waiting to be sliced and diced, Lura pulled up a stool and sat, twisting the unlucky orange vegetable like a washcloth.

"Okay, young lady, you know my kitchen rules. You come in my kitchen you better be working, eatin' or just passin' through."

"Sorry Lenni, I just wanted a nibble," came the soft reply as she relented and began to chew at the carrot stick.

"Humm sounds like you need more than a nibble, girl. What's wrong? You been cooped up in that room of yours since ya got here. Not answering the door and when ya do someone loses a head. You got man problems? Or should I ask if you got Whoa-men problems?" the older woman asked with a sharp twinkle in her hazel eye.

"Wha...what did you say, Lenni?" Lura stammered, almost choking on her carrot stick.

"Listen youngin, I have known you since your Mama and Papa brought you home. Plus I wasn't born last night, ya know. You been upset ever since you got home and left that tall, long legged, dark haired soldier gal I saw you all cozy with on TV. What'd she do that's got you all upset?"

The cook had not even glanced up nor missed a stroke on the chopping block. Lura smiled sadly and felt her shoulders sag,

"She left me, Lenni. She just up and left. There was a note on my pillow one morning and she was gone." Her voice choked on the last bit.

"Well, what did the note say, lovie?"

"Just that she didn't want to hurt anyone so she was leaving and she would love me...forever." Lura stared out the window, twisting the carrot stick until it snapped. She stared at the two broken pieces, surprised when a warm tear fell onto her hand. *I though I was over all that crying business* she thought.

Lenni glanced up at the snap of the carrot stick. *This child is really hurtin'. I hope her Mama's plans aren't gonna hurt her worse.* "Tell me bout' your soldier, child."

Lenni listened as Lura explained all that had happened in the last few months. The deaths she had witnessed, her own personal trials and the surprise she felt when she discovered the famous 'Desert Hawk' was a woman. Shyly she told of the beautiful, fierce soldier that had saved her life and stolen her heart. In halting tones she relived the horror of watching the woman she loved, fall in a hail of bullets. She spoke of the personal pain she had suffered watching her as she fought her way back to health. Finally, in tears and broken words, she told Lenni how her soldier had struggled, fighting an unseen enemy and herself to control the nightmares that haunted her even now, in the bright light of day.

"I just want to be with her Lenni. She needs me; she just doesn't know it. And...and I need her. I feel like there is a giant hand squeezing my heart and there is no relief in sight." Lura tucked her head, her small fist still wrapped around the broken carrot stick, clutched at her chest in an effort to stop the pain.

"Why would she leave me Lenni? I love her so much."

"Now you listen here, Ms. Lura. That soldier gal loves you. She just needs some time to get her head on and then you watch, she'll come a looking for ya. You can bet on that. She just don't strike me as the kind that would give up something she wants, and you, baby girl, are what she wants. You just give her some time." Lura still sat staring at the mutilated vegetable, not really hearing anything.

"Yeah, she loves me," she said. Sighing, she stood, tossing the orange remains into the trash bin as she left, her mind a thousand miles away.

Lenni's gaze followed her, shaking her head at the sad figure walking out the door. "That poor child, that woman of hers better get it together quick before her Mama is done with her planning." Lenora dropped her graying head back down and continued making the salad.

Alison Gillum-Grant sat at her antique Edwardian

writing desk in her private day room finishing the list of guests. She had her daughter home and it was time to get down to some serious arrangements. After a quick review of the social registrar, she was sure she had the names of the most eligible bachelors of the Richmond 500. Now all she needed was to contact the caterer, the decorator and talk that hardheaded daughter of hers into a dress. She had already had her year of running free, it was time to settle down with a nice young lawyer, or doctor and give her some grandchildren.

She ran the last stamp on the wet sponge and glued it precisely onto the corner of the cream colored invitation and with a nod of approval added it to the stack waiting to be posted.

In the foothills of the Blue Ridge Mountains, the silence of the late night was broken by a scream.

She watched as her finger pulled the trigger, the man she was aiming at stared in surprise as half his head exploded in a red burst, splattering his brains on the wall. Glancing up she saw skull fragments imbedded in the ceiling.

A sound to her right caught her attention, a young boy struggling with a dark man in robes. He was the only thing standing between the man and the fallen body of an old woman.

She felt her finger squeeze again but nothing happened. She threw the useless weapon aside and reached into her boot for her knife. Diving for the man she felt her body impact and tangle in his long robes. They struggled until she finally straddled him, her knife now protruding from his chest like a tiny third arm. She backed away from the quivering body but the robes held her bound to him. She struggled, fighting against the cloth but it had taken on a life of its own and wrapped itself around her tighter and tighter. It suffocated, her filling her mouth and lungs, choking her, wrapping around her throat. She struggled, fighting the cloth, falling and falling and falling.

"Dylan? Wake up! Dylan? It's only a bad dream, wake up!"

Her eyes opened to the gentle light of the moon streaming into her window. Her grandfather knelt beside her as she realized she was laying on the floor tangled in her own sheets.

"Grandfather?" Her voice came out in a whispering croak. She struggled with the sheets but her own body sweat caused them to cling to her exhausted body. She crawled like a small child to her grandfather, throwing her arms around his neck as the torrent of tears streamed down her cheeks. Her chest heaved with great gasps of air as the anguished filled sobs racked her still weak body.

Finally, the crying subsided and Gray Hawk helped the emotionally drained woman back into the bed. Covering her with fresh sheets and blankets he left her for a moment to heat up the kettle for tea. Returning to the tiny bedroom he slid the chair from the desk by the window next to the bed. Sitting down he took her cold trembling hand in his own as he stared into the vacant blue eyes.

"Dylan, can you tell me about the dream?" he asked, anxiety in his voice. At first he didn't hear her, but as he leaned closer she repeated her softly spoken word.

"So much blood, so many dead. I killed them, I

killed them all. My fault, my fault." The words were full of self-loathing and pain; the long slender hand trembled in his own.

The whistle of the kettle pulled him away from her, but he returned minutes later with a large cup of hot tea. Sitting again in the chair he held the cup as Dylan sipped the bittersweet liquid. Having taken in as much as she could, she lay back and stared up seeing again the deep red stain that dripped like macabre paint from the stucco ceiling. Her eyes grew heavy and she felt her mind slip into oblivion.

Gray Hawk stared down at his granddaughter, his forehead wrinkled in concern. Her spirit was in danger. He knew that she had many trails to travel before she would be safe. He was just not sure if she would be strong enough to travel it alone.

Dylan woke to the smell of fresh coffee and cooked bacon. Her head was clear but her heart was heavy. Climbing slowly from the bed, she slipped on a pair of socks and dressed in her dark blue shorts and gray sleeveless t-shirt and headed out to find the source of the intriguing smell. Down the hall and around the corner she found the kitchen with her grandfather stirring up a golden pan of scrambled eggs. She paused long enough to evaluate the older man.

He stood straight and tall, in his sweat pants and a white t-shirt, his lanky, muscular body belying his age. He had braided his silver hair into two long braids that hung over his chest, each wrapped in bright red cloth. Dylan remembered back to the days of her childhood when she had watched him slowly braid then wrap his hair. It had been black as a raven's wing then, the blue highlights glowing in the sun. He had taught her how to braid and had given her two strips of leather died bright blue to tie to the ends of her own glossy plaits.

Dylan smiled as she watched him scoop the hot breakfast onto a plate and place it on the small white kitchen table. "Good morning, Granddaughter, did I pass inspection and did you sleep well?" Dylan was startled, she had not made a sound and she did not see her grandfather look up.

"Umm, yes Grandfather, thank you. And you are not fooling me; you slipped me a 'mickey' last night in my tea. You are a very sneaky individual, you know that?" she said, attempting to be stern with the old man who had an annoying ability of being one of the few people who could ignore her anger and not fear retribution.

"Not last night Dylan, two nights ago. You have been sleeping for two full days and two full nights." Dylan felt the air leave her lungs, and her heart thumped in her ears. She had been asleep for forty-eight hours! How could that be?

"But…but, Grandfather how, why, what…?"

"Hush Dylan," the old man said, "you know the answers to all those questions. The simple truth is your body needed the rest; I just gave it a little help. Now sit down and eat," he added sternly, placing a heaping plate of food down on the table in front of her.

She did feel better having really slept for the first time in several days. Sitting down on the wooden chair by the food, she gazed down at the steaming plate, feeling, for the first time since leaving Lura, the gnawing bite of hunger. With her grandfather sitting nearby and looking on, she devoured the bacon, eggs and toast in minutes, then gulped down the still hot coffee, surprising herself with her appetite. Finally finishing her meal, she sat back and enjoyed the feeling of a full stomach. Dylan knew that the questions were coming. She knew and she dreaded them.

"Granddaughter, you are well now? You have healed from your injuries?" he asked, stirring another scoop of cream into a steaming cup of coffee. He sat in front of Dylan, carefully examining the dissolving cream, not even looking up.

"Yes Grandfather, my body has healed but..." Her voice choked as she thought of the nightmares, her eyes staring at her hands, looking for the blood stains.

"But what Granddaughter? Do you fear the memories, the dreams, the dead? They cannot hurt you. You have no reason to fear them."

"But Grandfather, I have killed so many, so many..." Her voiced cracked as she slid her hands from the table, hiding them from view. She hung her head in shame as the tears fell again.

"Granddaughter? Dylan...Dylan, did you kill innocent people? Did you kill in pleasure or for enjoyment? Did you enjoy the thrill?" he asked in a quiet calm voice, waiting for Dylan to respond.

"NO!! Never! I could not kill for the pleasure of killing." Dylan felt her stomach rebelling at the thoughts of the dead men. "At first, there was much I did not remember. I had many injuries and it took time to heal. I hated the men responsible for what happened to my unit and I wanted to kill them all," she said in a hard bitter voice.

"One day in a small village I was fighting, I saw one of the villagers shoot one of the raiders that had just fired on a woman running with her child. He fell at my feet…he was a boy. No more than 15 or 16, just a child killing children. It was as if someone hit me in the stomach with a board. I fell to my knees, crying. I have no idea why I wasn't shot that day, but after that, it became harder and harder. I couldn't stand to see the villages attacked, but every shot I fired I knew I had killed someone's child." Dylan's voice spoke softly; she stared at her hands again expecting to see the blood of the men whose lives she had ended.

"When you killed these men, were you fighting?" the old warrior asked in a quiet steady voice. He sipped his coffee, his eyes still focused on the creamy brown liquid.

"Yes Grandfather, whenever I heard of the fighting, I would come and…and stop them. Some times I would lure them to a village with the rumor of hidden weapons or money. They would come into the village and I would be there…waiting," she finished quietly, her eyes glazed over as she remembered.

Her grandfather sat quietly contemplating her comments, still staring at his coffee. "So you killed to protect? You protected the helpless? The women and children? And you protected yourself? And you feel there is no honor in that, Granddaughter? Would you rather they had been left alone to be killed or raped? You rather they had killed you?"

"NO! Yes! I don't know, I don't know…" she cried, tears streaming down her cheeks.

"Granddaughter, think of what you have told me. You killed to protect the innocent and to protect yourself. The people you killed had slaughtered your unit. They had killed many innocent people. They would not have thought twice of putting a bullet through you. Yet you agonize over their deaths?

Remember this, Dylan; they were killers. If they claimed to be soldiers, they knew what they were doing. All who kill for a living know the consequences of their actions. These were not needy people. They were not defending their homes or families. They were not honorable warriors. These "soldiers", these "men", were not human, they were less than animals. They destroyed everything they touched not for their loved ones, not for their country. They did it for themselves, for the sake of their own greed. They needed to beat down the people to make themselves feel tall. There is no honor in that. You saw this injustice. You could have joined them and lived off of the anguish of the people. Would you feel better then?"

Dylan did not raise her head just shook it slowly.

"Granddaughter, you were the only thing between death and the people. As long as you were there they could not succeed and the people lived. These men were evil, taking all they could, destroying what they could not take. They would have destroyed you if they could. Do not let them win now in death what they could not win in life." The old man quietly collected the dirty dishes and placed them in a sink of hot soapy water then turned and walked out.

Dylan thought about the words of her Grandfather and she knew he was right. The men she had killed were terrorists. They made a living by taking whatever they could from the innocent people around them. They claimed to be soldiers and they knew the possible consequences of their actions.

Still mulling over these words, Dylan returned to her room and changed into her running gear.

It was morning again. Lura rolled out of bed and shuffled into the bathroom. Looking into the mirror she saw a pale face surrounded by ruffled dull hair and sad eyes.

I have got to pull myself together. I look like poop. Heck, I feel like poop. Maybe I need to get out, go for a run or something. A bit of fresh air to help clear my head might help. Hell, maybe I will get lucky and get hit by a truck. At least if I am unconscious maybe I can get some sleep.

Sighing she turned and went back to her room. Reaching the dresser she opened the top drawer and pulled out a pair of running shorts, a pair of jock socks and a sports bra, closing this she opened the second drawer and selected a black shirt. Slipping out of her nightshirt she slid the shorts on over her panties and pulled on the bra and black top. Sitting back on the bed she pulled on the socks and slipped her feet into her running shoes. Still sitting there she stared down at her shoes, her mind a million miles away. Finally she stood, gathered her energy and headed out of her room and down the stairs. She crossed the hall, passed the foyer and stepped out the front door. The wind and the cool air immediately reminded her that she was in Northern Virginia and fall was definitely in the air. Trotting down the long stairs she jogged down the driveway, across the lawn and out the front gate.

An hour later she returned, sweat pouring off of her and her breath coming in ragged gasps. She staggered up the front stairs and into the house, exhausted and no closer to understanding her feelings than when she had started out. She leaned against the front door thinking about Dylan, why had she left and where was she. *I know she loves me.* Deep in thought, she didn't hear her mother calling to her.

"Lura, Lura honey where are you? Lura? Oh, there you are. Goodness dear, you are half naked and covered with perspiration; I hope you didn't go out in public dressed like that. People can see... well almost everything and what they can't see I am sure they can provide from their dirty little minds. What were you thinking parading around with your legs exposed like that, and where in the world did you find those clothes?"

Lura finally realized that she was wearing a pair of Dylan's gray Army shorts and a black and gold Pembroke State University shirt. It was Dylan's favorite. She rubbed her hand across the raised lettering trying to feel closer to her soulmate when what her mother was saying finally sank in.

"What? What did you say, Mother?"

"I said that you need to go upstairs and get cleaned up then get some rest. We are having a small social get together tonight and I want you looking fresh."

"Oh, sure, alright." Lura turned, her thoughts miles away, and headed towards the stairs. "Whoa, wait a minute, what do you mean a 'social gathering'?" she asked, turning to face her mother

"Well, yes dear, I have invited some of my dear friends over for a small party and they are bringing their children. I hope you will not embarrass me by staying in your room or presenting yourself in those disgusting blue jeans you are so fond of wearing."

"Mother, back off. I am not in the mood to argue with you over clothes and if this little get together of yours is a hen party to set me up with one of your friends eligible mutant sons, forget it."

"Now you listen to me young lady," her mother interjected. "You promised that if we gave you time to try out this 'working thing' you would come home and settle down. Well, it has been a year. It is now time for you to find someone socially acceptable and settle down. No more of this gallivanting all over the world with strange persons and getting shot at. My goodness, what were you thinking?"

I was thinking about a wonderful woman with beautiful long legs and eyes to die for but if I told you that you would just flip out Lura thought

"Alright, I will attend your little head hunting session, Mother, but I will not, and hear me loud and clear on this, I will not be paraded out like a prize filly for any man there." She turned and climbed up the stairs, ignoring the ranting of the woman below.

Dylan returned from her run feeling exhausted but clean. The run had burned much of the self-hatred and doubt from her mind, at least for the moment. All that was left was the confusion of her memories. Would she still be haunted by memories?

"Grandfather? Grandfather?" she called running from room to room, calling to the old man.

"I am here Dylan and though I am old, I am not deaf" the old man responded entering from the kitchen, his arms loaded with firewood. Dylan rushed forward to relieve the senior of his burden carrying the wood to the fireplace, neatly stacking part of it and arranging several small logs over some kindling. She reached for the long matches to light the fire.

"Grandfather, I have been thinking…"

"Well, it's about time you stopped moping and started using that brain the Great Spirit gave you," the old man whispered under his breath.

"What was that, Grandfather?" Dylan asked, knowing that there was nothing wrong with her hearing either and smiling at the remark she had overheard.

"Oh nothing Dylan. What did you need? I heard you calling like a wounded wolf."

"Well, I have thought about what you said earlier about…about the men I…I killed." Dylan glanced down at her hands expecting them to be covered with blood. "I have tried to remember all of the men. Thinking of each one at a time. I cannot think of one that was an innocent, not one who did not already have blood on their hands. Those men, the ones I killed were all soldiers. You are right; they knew what might happen, they understood the laws of the warrior. Some fought with honor, most did not. I will not carry their spirits on my shoulders any longer, but I cannot understand why my mind returns to the desert, to the killing. I have lost control of my thoughts. I am no longer safe around my family, my friends, the woman I…"

She stopped her and raised her eyes to meet those of her mentor. "The woman I love," she said strongly, tilting her head back and her blue eyes sparkling in challenge.

"Do not stare at me in challenge Little Hawk. I can still put you over my knee," the old man said in a stern voice.

71

"I am sorry Grandfather, it is just that…well it is so… argh! My brain is in knots!"

"Dylan, I have known you since the day your mother brought you home screaming and fighting because they wanted to put you in diapers and even then you rebelled. Funniest thing I ever saw. All you had to do to keep you from crying was let you run around buck naked." He smiled, watching the faint red creep up the young woman's cheeks.

Then in a serious tone he told her, "I have known ever since the first trip with the young warriors that you were touched by the Great Spirit and blessed with the spirit of the hawk. I knew then that no man would tame you. What is she like, this woman who has tamed the hawk?"

Dylan smiled at her grandfather, her heart and eyes filled with love she told him about her falcon.

Standing by the fireplace in the large formal living room Lura resembled a burning emerald in a deep green satin tea gown. The front was cut low revealing the golden skin, still tanned from the desert sun. The back was cut even lower, accentuating a slim waist and strong back. Matching deep green sling back shoes finished the outfit and a slender gold chain with a single large deep green emerald graced her throat, her ears were pierced with matching emerald studs.

Glancing around the room her eyes skipped over each handsome, perfect male face and she categorized the young male members of the party into three distinct categories: No, Never and Not as Long as there is Breath in my Body.

There is really a fourth category she thought, *but I*

*am definitely keeping that one to myself. It's the 'They could never hold a candle to Dylan' Category. They **all** fall into that category.*

Sighing aloud she lifted her glass of ginger ale and sipped. She never had acquired a taste for champagne, it always seemed to give her a headache. Her eyes returned again to the room, scanning the faces of the men as they laughed, making bold gestures in an attempt to draw her attention.

"Just like a bunch of strutting roosters. The one that crows loudest is the one that gets the hens."

She smiled, her mind slipping to the gutter for a minute as she thought, *It's just that this hen doesn't like cocks. Oh that was bad! Naughty, naughty Lura, shame on you.* she smiled as she sipped again silently on her drink in a vain attempt to hide her chuckle. *Ginger ale tastes great down the throat, but heaven help you if it comes out your nose.*

"Is there something you would like to share with us, dear?" a voice sounded at her elbow.

Lura inhaled, startled at the voice and even more so to realize it was her mother. The ginger ale that mere moments ago had acted as a helpful disguise now rushed its chilling way down her windpipe and up into her sinuses. Her eyes bulged as she coughed, choking on the bubbly drink. Her mother patted her gently on the back, a useless gesture since it did not carry the strength she needed to knock the breath back into her lungs. Finally gathering herself she turned to face her parent, her hand still covering her mouth, her eyes watering from the recent fit.

"Mother, you startled me." *Boy is that the understatement of the year* she thought, still catching her breath. "What can I do for you?"

"Well, dear, if you are sure you are okay?" her mother questioned.

"Yes, mother, I am fine." Lura replied, already frustrated with the small woman.

"Well, then, let me introduce to you Mr. Nathan Bedford Owens the Third. His mother and I attended the University of Virginia together, we are sorority sisters."

Lura turned to smile at the young man that her mother was presenting, her mind vaguely catching the rather formal introduction her mother was making.

"Nathan, this is my lovely daughter, Victoria Lura Gillum-Grant," she said. *Finally my daughter is meeting the proper people and Nathan is from such fine stock. I hope she has the sense to see what a wonderful opportunity this is for her. My, she is just speechless with pleasure* Alison thought.

Lura, felt the smile freeze on her face as the hairs on her neck rose. Her eyes made contact with those of the young man and a shiver ran involuntarily down her spine. He gazed at her with cold dark eyes that seemed to undress her and assess her all in one glance. She quickly withdrew the hand she had raised to his, instead using it to brush an imaginary strand of hair from her eyes.

"Mr. Owens," she said, her voice chilled and the smile finally gone from her face. She did not like this man. She was not sure why but she knew there was something not quite right. Her internal alarms were sounding and she had learned long ago, when dealing with men, to listen to those alarms.

"Ms. Grant, it is a real pleasure, your mother has told me so much about you." Nathan bowed his sleek head a thatch of blond hair fell forward giving him a rakish appearance which he knew most women found devilishly attractive.

This man is dangerous that is what is setting off my systems Lura thought.

"Funny, she has never mentioned you, Mr. Owens," Lura stated coldly. "Please excuse me, I must go freshen up," she said as she turned away and headed towards the stairs.

"I am so sorry, Nathan. I have no idea what has come over her. She has just not been herself since she returned from that dreadful experience overseas," Alison gasped in an effort to smooth ruffled feathers.

"I understand completely, Mrs. Grant. Perhaps you would allow me the opportunity to provide your daughter with a distraction. Would it be possible to stop by tomorrow and perhaps take her for a ride in the country?"

"That sounds like a wonderful idea, Nathan. It may just be what Lura needs to snap her out of her little doldrums," Alison added with a smile.

My God, what is mother thinking? Doesn't she have any idea what kind of man that is? I know a predator when I see one, and that guy is a shark! Lura stepped into the bathroom and leaned against the sink, her back to the mirror and her arms folded.

"Dylan baby, I love you, but I am gonna give you such a thump on the head when I find you for leaving me in this situation."

Lura sighed, stood up straight, brushed the front of her tea gown, squared her shoulders and turned to march back out into battle.

Dylan sighed as she sipped her coffee; her grandfather had always been an understanding sort and had always supported her. He seemed to be fascinated by Lura. The conversation had distracted her from her morose thoughts but now she reluctantly remembered the reason she had left the beautiful blonde.

"Grandfather, I am troubled," she began, "Twice now I have reacted on reflex to situations and both times I have come close to harming someone who was completely innocent." Dylan remembered Lura's expression when the coffee spilled down the front of her robe and the terrified expression of fear on the face of the young Frisbee player. "I can't seem to stop myself, I react without thought. I am afraid..." She stopped here unable to voice her thoughts.

"Yes, you are afraid of what, Dylan? That you will hurt someone innocent? Dylan nodded in silence.

Humm, I understand," Gray Hawk whispered. He leaning forward resting his elbows on his knees, a gesture his Granddaughter unconsciously mirrored. "You have been through much in the last few years, perhaps it is time you took a little vacation," the old man whispered.

"Huh? But Grandfather, I have been on vacation ever since I returned to the United States, I am sick of vacation. Maybe if I go back to work..."

"No Dylan, that is not the sort of vacation I mean. Ever since you returned you have lost yourself. You have not had the chance to stop and touch the earth. I believe it is time for you to go on a vision quest."

CHAPTER 7

The day stretched into late afternoon and Dylan strolled at her grandfather's side, enjoying the brisk air and the sound of leaves crackling under her sneakers. The trees were beginning to shed their green coat in favor of the colorful gold and red of fall. This was an ancient forest; the tall and gnarled trees had dropped their dead leaves and a few branches that were the size of small trees themselves. Dylan paused as one rather large tree cracked. She glanced up just as a thick branch, the size of a sapling, fell at her feet.

"Cedar," she said, "I love the smell of cedar." She bent and retrieved the broken limb that was nearly as long as she was tall. Snapping off the shorter, dead limbs she continued down the path following the old warrior.

"Okay, Grandfather, I know that you have some plan in mind. I trust you, I really do, but I am not sure about this 'quest' business. If I remember correctly, young braves went on a vision quest to discover their destiny and learn of their totem animals. Do you really think that going into the forest and starving myself into unconsciousness is going to help?" Dylan asked, becoming frustrated. Her grandfather had spent the better part of the morning gathering some of her clothes, a first aid kit and a minimum of food, stuffing it all into a large backpack. He also seemed to have suddenly become completely deaf. He went from room to room gathering items and shoving them into the pack all the while humming a disjointed tune that sounded strangely enough like an ancient lullaby that her grandmother had sung to her on long stormy nights.

"Dylan." The old man paused and turned to the young soldier. "The vision quest is not just a trip into the woods to starve yourself; it is a journey of discovery. While you are there you will find out which totem animals guide your life and are the key to your destiny. You may learn where you future lies and ways to control the memories of your past."

Dylan frowned, she had always believed in her grandfather and she knew that he had powers that were mysterious to say the least, but she was still skeptical about the ability of animals to guide her future. However if there was one person in her life, one person besides Lura, who could convince her to go on a quest, it was this wise old man.

"Okay, Grandfather, I will go. What do I need to do?"

"Nothing, Granddaughter. Well, nothing yet. Let's go home and I will fix you a nice meal. We can talk more then," the old man replied. He watched Dylan strip the small branches off of the limb and start to use it as a walking stick.

They turned and headed back down the trail towards the large cabin. Dylan paused at the door to throw the branch away, then turned and entered the cabin. Her grandfather smiled quietly as he followed the tall soldier into the warm interior.

"Mother, I have no intention of going anywhere with that pompous ass Nathan! He is as thickheaded, bias and chauvinistic as they come and I am not so sure he is interested in a wife. What makes you think that I would even give that wanker the time of day?" Lura ranted as she paced back and forth on the plush eggshell white carpet in her bedroom, waving her arms about for emphasis.

"Victoria Lura Gillum-Grant! I am your mother and you will watch your mouth when you speak to me. You lower your tone right this minute!" Alison yelled back. She was shocked and appalled at the terms her gently raised daughter was using. She certainly did not learn them at home.

It never occurred to Alison Grant that her daughter certainly had learned those terms at home. She spent many a day on her Daddy's knee listening while he conducted business and Harrison Grant was never one to bite his tongue. Bite off a head or two yes, but his tongue, never. It seemed that though she got her blond haired green-eyed good looks from her mother, Lura definitely inherited her father's temper and colorful repertoire.

Lura winced, knowing that she may have stepped just a bit too close to the edge for her mother. Taking a deep breath, she tried again.

"Mother please, you can't be serious. Nathan is a snake and you know how I feel about snakes," she added under her breath for good measure. She turned and faced her mother, her green eyes large and pleading.

Don't even try that puppy dog look on me Lura, you know it doesn't work," Alison said as she turned and walked towards her daughter's large walk-in closet. She peeled back the door to reveal a long narrow room lined on both sides with every imaginable style dress, slacks, shoes, boots, and of course evening wear. She sniffed as she passed an open suitcase containing three faded pairs of Levi's, one pair of well-worn hiking boots, a pair of sneakers and a large assortment of t-shirts. She made a mental note to tell the upstairs maid to remove those atrocious garments right away. She smiled, remembering that the gardener was raking up the first fall of leaves and thought those horrid pants would make wonderful kindling.

She walked past the dresses and went through the racks of expensive slacks selecting a pair of camel tan business slacks and a deep green turtle neck sweater. She continued to thumb through the clothes until she found a dark brown tweed jacket, brown short boots and a matching leather belt. Laying all these on the bed she turned placed her small fists on her girlishly slender hips and glared at her child.

"Now what?" Lura asked throwing her arms in the air in a fit of exasperation. Her mother simply pointed to the bath and began tapping her foot. Feeling suspiciously like a six year old caught with muddy britches, Lura hung her head in resignation and headed for the tub.

Hours later Lura found herself belted into the front seat of a sporty bright red BMW 330Ci Convertible Coupe racing at breakneck speed down the drive of her family's estate. She stared out the front windscreen fully expecting to see her life pass before her eyes. She gripped the center console with one hand and the leather wrapped door armrest with the other. Apparently the pompous ass only knew one speed… fast as hell.

"Umm Nathan, the drive ends here. Don't you think you should slow down a bit? The road turns really sharply at the end," Lura gasped in a frightened voice.

"Aw Lura, where is your sense of adventure? I know you have lived a sheltered life, but allow a bit of excitement into it every once in a while, will you," Nathan stated, smiling in what he hoped was a debonair manner.

He hoped this little Virginia wallflower would not dampen his style after he married her. His family had a name and a place in society, but the finances were getting a bit slim and though the Grants were relatively new money, merely from the time of the Civil War, it would be an acceptable arrangement. He had hoped that Lura would be into a bit of excitement, but so far he had been very disappointed. Apparently this was a sheltered woman who would faint at the slightest bit of thrill.

Oh well, I suppose her parents will give us a small summerhouse as a wedding gift. I can put her there so she won't interfere with my life. She is passably attractive; I suppose we will breed nice children. Huh, as long as one is a male, then father's will would be satisfied and I can get my money he thought as he rounded the hairpin curve at the end of the drive.

He smiled at himself as he heard her gasp in alarm. *This may turn into a fun drive after all* he thought.

Gray Hawk carefully placed two steaming hot plates on the table. He had taken special care with this meal and intended make sure that Dylan filled up before she headed out on her quest. The steaks were large, thick and rare just like they both liked them. A pile of homemade mashed potatoes, fresh biscuits and a large pile of sweet yellow corn finished the food. Two tall sweating glasses of sweet iced tea provided the refreshment. He watched with a smile as Dylan's eyes grew large staring at the plate in front of her. "Dylan, it will not get to your stomach through your eyes," he stated with laughter in his voice

Dylan looked up and grinned, her grandfather always knew how to make her smile and boy, steak could put a smile on her face faster than a crispy French fry.

She picked up her fork and knife and dug in. They ate in silence, each humming and groaning over every bite until the plate was clean. Dylan sat back, rubbing her aching belly and eyed the senior.

"Okay, Grandfather, why are you feeding me like the fatted calf? Not that I am complaining mind you. Just...curious," Dylan commented, adding a smile to ease the bite of her words.

"Well Granddaughter, since you will be leaving on your quest tomorrow and living off the land, I thought it best to make sure you had a good meal in you to live on for a bit," he commented, still staring at his plate while chasing the last yellow kernel of corn around with his fork.

Dylan smiled and thought about what her

grandfather had just said. She remembered the summer they had spent in the forest with the young men of the tribe earning the rights of the warrior. She looked back and thought of those almost carefree days of her youth. Her mind envisioned the younger Dylan competing with the young men, challenging them, nature and her own young body. Learning to live off the land had helped her survive for years in the desert. There was little she did not know about survival and, she thought with a grim smile, little she could not handle. She glanced again at her grandfather, smiling as he finally captured the sweet tidbit and popped it triumphantly into his mouth.

"Thank you for the wonderful meal Grandfather. I am sure my belly will be content for many days to come. Now, how about moving into the living room so we can talk?"

CHAPTER 8

Lura slammed the door of the BMW coupe.

"Nathan, I don't want to ever see you or hear your irritating voice again. I have no clue what gave your poor excuse for a brain the idea that I would allow you any liberties! And as far as your thoughts of marriage are concerned, if we were the last two humans on the planet then the human race would be in deep shit because we would be the last two humans on the planet!"

On that note Lura turned on her heel and stomped her way up the stairs and into the house leaving Nathan fuming in the driveway. *Hell, I just wanted to give her the chance to sample the wares before we get married. This is all I need to be tied to a frigid woman for the rest of my life. You would think she would be happy to have any attention after she moved back home. My God, who would want a woman who has obviously been around? Maybe she's just looking for an excuse, yeah that has to be it, why else would she turn me down? Oh yeah, that has to be it. Well, then it looks like Ms. Grant may be a bit more of a challenge after all. Yep this is gonna be fun, well until we get married, then all that independent shit has to go.* Nathan slammed the gearshift into first and threw gravel down the drive as he sped off.

Lura was mad, no not just mad. Mad was just not a strong enough word; she was furious beyond comprehension. "How dare that overgrown, whiny assed excuse for a man try that with me?" she fumed, pacing back and forth in the foyer.

She had been invited to go for a drive into the country and had finally agreed to go after being pressured by her mother. They had no sooner reached the edge of town than Nathan decided to pull off, complaining of car trouble.

"If that isn't the oldest and lamest excuse in the book..."

He pulled over at the first rest stop and steered the little car into a secluded section of the parking lot. He then proceeded to extol Lura on his pedigree, his family wealth and last, but certainly least, his own personal "assets". He pulled her quickly to him and began to kiss her, trying to force his tongue past her clamped teeth while his hands were busy roughly squeezing her breast. *I really don't think he was expecting that punch to the gut but he really had it coming.* "He should be glad I am such a lady, if Dylan had been here... Dylan, where are you, love?"

As she strolled through the forest, Dylan's mind went back over the conversation she'd had with her grandfather before heading out.

"Now Dylan make sure you find a location that is open to the sky, you will know it is the right place when you see it. You must build a sweat hut, the sweat will help purify your mind and body." He stepped out the front door and returned an instant later with the long cedar stick she had found in the forest the day before. "Take this with you. As your spirit guides visit you must carve their names on it. It is powerful medicine and will protect you on your quests."

Dylan glided through the forest using the stick to move aside small branches and to steady her steps as she crossed streams. She remembered that her grandfather had also carried such a staff when he had taken her and the young men of their village on their summer excursions. He had called it his totem stick and told tales of the four animals whose names had been carved on it. *I liked the tales of the wily fox the best* she thought smiling.

The forest was cool and a soft breeze pushed at her back, encouraging her to move on. The trail she was following was narrow but clear; the hoof prints that marked the trail were those of a large buck. Dylan bent to check the fresh spoor she found on the edge of the path, smiling at the knowledge that the forest skills her grandfather had taught her so long ago were coming back to her. Standing, she looked around at the bright, clear Carolina blue sky and inhaled the crisp, clean smell of the evergreens. The Blue Ridge Mountains were beautiful this time of year, the leaves were just beginning to change color and the forest was dressed in shades of gold, yellow, scarlet and green. She had been on the march since early morning and gauging from the location of the sun it was approaching noon. She would have to stop soon and eat. She looked around for a likely place to rest and noticing a smaller path off of the main trail, she turned to follow it.

Alison Grant heard the disturbance in her foyer and followed the sounds. She reached the main hall and saw her daughter pacing, her arms flailing in the air and her agitated voice rose to a level that echoed in her pristine entry.

"Lura, what in the name of heaven are you doing? Lower your voice, lower it this instant young lady. Proper ladies do not raise their voices above the conversational tone, proper young ladies maintain their composure and..."

Before she could go any further, her young progeny interrupted her. "Mother, 'proper young ladies' do not have to mace their dates to save their virtue!" she exclaimed. "That...that... that person you had me go out with nearly raped me in the parking lot of the rest stop on I-95!" Lura stated indignantly. She was still fuming over her educational ride with Nathan.

"But Lura dear, he seemed like such a nice young man. He comes from an old Virginia family, is well spoken and well educated. Couldn't you be mistaken?"

"NO! Mother, Nathan is a slimy, disgusting multi-armed excuse for a man. And, make no mistake about this mother, I WILL NOT under any circumstances go anywhere with him again." On that note she turned and, still mumbling under her breath, headed for the stairs.

Alison stood there for a moment watching her daughter stomp up the stairs muttering to herself the entire way. The younger woman turned down the long hall and disappeared. Moments later she was startled by the slamming of a bedroom door.

"Well, that went better than I expected," came an amused voice behind her. Alison whipped around and saw her husband standing in the doorway of his office, leaning against the frame.

"What do you mean, Harrison? Lura offended that young man and has refused to see him again. How are we suppose to find her a suitable young man if she behaves that way?" Alison asked, turning angry green eyes on her spouse.

"We aren't going to find her a 'suitable young man' because our daughter has already found someone," Harrison stated, folding his long arms across a barrel chest.

"What do you mean, she has already found someone? She hasn't been out of the house since she got back from that dreadful trip to that horrid desert country," Alison stated, her hands now firmly planted on her hips.

"Well, if I remember correctly, our daughter came home with a young soldier. And if I am not mistaken, she spent quite a bit of time with that same soldier in the desert and in the hospital. Seems our daughter has already fallen in love." Harrison grinned watching as reality finally dawned on his wife.

"No, you mean to tell me that our daughter is, is...one of them?" She gasped, her hand at her throat.

Harrison frowned at his wife, he had not realized that she was homophobic, but understanding that she did come from an old Southern family he was not really surprised.

This time he took the aggressive stance. With his fists balled up and placed firmly on his hips he glared at his wife. "What exactly do you mean, 'one of them'? Our daughter has always had good judgment when it comes to people and if she has decided that this woman is who she wants to spend her life with, then so be it," he bellowed. "That soldier saved our daughter's life. Had she not been there we would have lost Lura, so as far as I am concerned, if that is what Lura wants then that is what Lura will have, and you and I will support her. I love my daughter and if this is her decision, then we will stand by her one hundred percent!" On that note, he turned back to his office and, like his daughter, slammed the door, leaving Alison standing gape jawed in the foyer.

Down the hall in the kitchen a soft click was heard as the kitchen door quietly shut. "Well, I didn't think he had it in him, I thought that wife of his neutered him years ago," Lenni chuckled. "Hmm, seems that nearly losing that little gal woke up that old bear. So Miss Lura may have a chance with that soldier gal of hers after all." Lenni smiled and hummed to herself as she returned to the kitchen to finish the dinner preparations.

CHAPTER 9

Nathan turned into the drive of his family home, the house that had been the home of the Owens family for five generations. To those not familiar with the estate, it looked palatial. The huge Georgian pillars, white and majestic supported the front portion of the entry, the giant double oak doors, the winding gravel and brick drive and the beautiful green lawn dotted here and there with flowering shrub, all the picture of Southern charm. But Nathan noticed the tarnished brass of the oaken door's handles, the drawn blinds which hid the missing furniture, sold a year ago to pay debts, and the dead flower beds that once housed a variety of beautiful plants and flowering bushes, gone along with the gardener.

All this will be restored just as soon as I marry the little twit Grant Nathan thought. *And I will marry her. Then I will restore the estate and plant her in it. Once she is pregnant, I will have fulfilled my obligations and then I can do as I please. With her money and mine I can fix the place up and then travel. Germany is beautiful this time of year.* Nathan chuckled to himself as he pressed the button to open the garage and slide the BMW in next to the classic old 1964 Rolls Royce sedan. It would have gone too except it did not run and the cost of repairs made fixing it out of the question.

Plus, it will look great once I get it fixed and hire a driver, Nathan smirked.

He shut the car door and skirted around the old car and entered the house. He strolled through the mudroom and into the kitchen, glancing around he imagined the cooking staff snapping to attention at his presence. Smiling to himself he walked to the large aluminum covered refrigerator and opened the freezer compartment, removing a store brand frozen meal. He crossed the kitchen to the microwave. Reaching into a drawer along the counter he pulled out a fork and, after poking holes in the plastic covering the meal, he tossed it into the oven and slammed the door. Adjusting the timer to four minutes he leaned back against the cooking island with his arms folded across his chest, deep in thought. His mind was picturing the changes he was going to make and the clubs he would be able to return to with the money he would finally inherit after the marriage produced an heir, combined with the money his new wife would bring.

Yes life is definitely looking up, he thought as the bell on the oven rang.

Having refreshed herself with a cool drink from her canteen, Dylan rose and began walking again. The trail she followed was faint and she suspected that it was a deer trail, but her instinct told her it was also the right path for her vision quest.

What exactly am I suppose to discover on this quest? I have no idea where I am going or why in the hell I am doing this, but it feels right. I know that I am going where I need to be, I just hope I figure out what I am suppose to do once I get there. Using her walking staff to part the hanging vines and overgrown tree branches she continued on her path, drawn as if on a tether towards an unknown location.

Pushing aside the last prickly branch from her path Dylan found herself in a small clearing, and what she saw took her breath away. In front of her was a huge cedar tree, its branches full and heavy with green. Around the base of the tree were fallen needles and debris in all shades from dark green to golden mahogany. The ancient tree was the only thing in the clearing; the other trees around and beyond the giant seemed to have retreated leaving this old monarch standing alone in its space. The ground was covered with soft dark emerald green moss. Tiny white flowers spotted the moss giving it a surreal look. Dylan realized that she had reached the end of her search; this was where she would stay until her quest was complete.

Slipping her pack from her back, Dylan rolled her shoulders to relieve the tension then twisted her neck, smiling when she heard the soft pop of the vertebrate as they realigned themselves. She glanced around and then bent to remove a small hatchet from her pack. Whistling softly to herself she headed into the tree line to look for kindling and saplings for the sweat lodge.

Lura was not happy, it wasn't that she didn't like her mother, it wasn't that she didn't appreciate what her mother was doing, but what was driving her nuts was the driver her mom had procured. She loved shopping, she loved spending her mother's money, but what she hated was the fact that somehow Nathan had finagled his way into being their driver. Now she was stuck between her mother's efforts to pair her up with a man she was quickly beginning to hate and keeping Nathan out of groping range.

"Lura honey, could you come here please? I have got to see you in this dress," her mother called, holding up a strapless black dress. With a sigh of resignation Lura walked over and took the dress, turning full circle she finally located the dressing rooms and headed off that way.

Nathan watched as the blond stepped through the portal and down the short hall into a dressing booth. Thinking this might be his only opportunity for the day, he followed her.

Heh, Mama Grant is a real Godsend, for an old bat he thought, trying the handle of the dressing room door he had just seen Lura enter. The door swung open easily on its solid brass hinges and Nathan smiled with anticipation. *She is going to love this* he thought with a smile.

Dylan had just finished laying the last rock in the pit in the center of the sweat lodge, it had taken the majority of the afternoon to build but she was pleased with the construction. The lodge was actually more a hut, shaped much like an igloo with a small center hole, the door which pointed east was covered by a blanket.

The majority of the hut was made of bent saplings, canvas, mud and bits of leaves that she had gathered.

Inside, the Spirit Path was laid with stones leading from the opening to a small depression she had scooped out in the center of the path and directly under the hole in the roof. This she lined with more mud and large rocks. These would be heated, then water would be poured over them causing steam, the steam would cause her to sweat. That sweat would release the impurities from her body and carry her prayers into the sky. Inside the lodge Dylan lay four large logs, one in each direction: North, South, East and West. This final task completed, she left the lodge to relax before her ordeal. Tomorrow she would begin the cleansing ritual and heating the ancestor stones that were in her pack.

Now she needed to build her shelter for the evening then prepare dinner. This was to be the last food or drink she would have until after her vision quest.

The sound of flesh meeting flesh seemed to echo up and down the aisles of the store and spill out into the outer courts along the walk in front of the boutique. The stream of words accompanied by the slap seemed to travel even further.

Nathan was stunned; she had actually struck him. What was she thinking? He held his hand to his injured cheek and quickly exited the dressing area, Lura close on his heels.

"How dare you! What possessed that weak brain of yours that allowed you to assume I would welcome your slimy presence in my dressing room?" Lura roared, not caring who heard. Mrs. Grant was, for the first time in several years, speechless. She would never have presumed that Nathan was anything other than a gentleman. But to enter her daughters dressing room while she was unclothed? Oh n o, this would definitely not do.

"Nathan?" she asked calmly, "Am I to understand that you took it upon yourself to assist my Lura with her attire?" A brow was raised in inquiry over flashing gray green eyes.

Oh boy, this is not good. How was I to know the girl was a prude? Aloud he said, "Um, well, it was like this Mrs. Grant, I though I heard Lura call out to me and..."

"And you what?" the indignant matriarch asked, ice dripping from each coldly enunciated word. "You assumed my daughter was being attacked by the Armani? I am sorry, Mr. Owens, but it would appear that we are no longer in need of you assistance. Good day," Alison stated, coldly turning her back on Nathan, effectively dismissing him.

Nathan stood there, his mouth open as if gasping for air as he watched Alison and Lura Grant turn and re-enter the dressing room together. At the last minute, Lura turned as she reached the doorway of the dressing room and stuck her tongue out at Nathan. She knew it was childish but, *what the Hell, it felt good,* she thought smiling at her mother as she pulled her cell phone from her hip to call their regular driver.

Nathan balled his fists and groaned. His meal ticket was slipping though his fingers, he would have to do something quick. He reached into his pocket for his keys and stalked out of the store. He had some damage control to initiate. As he reached parking lot he glanced around for the BMW, pressing the alarm he waited for the horn to alert him to the location of the car.

"Damn mall parking, never can find the car," he muttered to himself. Just then he heard it, the high-pitched honking horn of his beautiful Coupe. Turning his head he watched in stunned amazement as a tow truck passed directly in front of him hauling away his prized sports car. The sign on the side of the truck read, "BIG RED's REPO – You call 'em, We haul 'em"

A huge light skinned black man waved at him from behind the wheel of the truck, a cigar butt clenched in his grinning white teeth.

Dylan sat on a log in front of the warm fire, her thoughts drifting to a woman, a little bit of a thing, with hair the color of the Indian corn, shades of gold and red and yellow all as fiery as the sun. *And a spirit to match,* she thought smiling. *Where was Lura right now? Was she okay?*

Her mind drifted back to their first night at home together. She had felt so bad and Lura had been so sweet, helping her out of the tub, carefully drying every part of her so tenderly. She was so exhausted her body trembled just trying to stand. Lura had wrapped the towel around her and led her to the bed.

Dylan shifted, sliding off the log to stretch her long legs out to enjoy the heat of the fire; she allowed her back to rest against the log.

Lura was so gentle that night; she had pulled the covers back and helped her slip into bed. She remembered how Lura had run around to the other side of the bed, stripping as she went, clothing flying in all directions. She had snuggled under the sheets, and for the first time since they had left the hospital, she curled naked around Dylan's long body. One bare leg was flung possessively over Dylan's thighs. Warm crisp curls brushed Dylan's hip and one soft white arm wrapped itself around her waist.

Smiling, Dylan remembered the smell of the blond head on her shoulder and the feel of the soft breasts pressing into her side. She had been unable to resist stroking the soft flesh so close at hand. One arm had wrapped around the smaller woman, pulling her closer into Dylan's embrace as long slender fingers had gently taken an erect nipple and rolled it between thumb and fingers. A soft moan escaped Lura's lips letting Dylan know that she was not quite as tired as she had been earlier. She remembered that they had made love slowly, gently that night and had fallen into an exhausted, but very satisfied, sleep.

She remembered the last time her hands had caressed the soft white breasts. That memory was sweet and painful because the next day was the last time she had seen Lura.

Sadly Dylan thought of the circumstances that had led her here, to this point in time, to this location. The fighting, the killing, and all the death. She was not fit to be with Lura. Dylan hung her head as silent tears burned their way down her cheeks.

Gray Hawke moved silently back through the forest, his head bowed in thought. He had known that Dylan would find this place for her vision quest; it was the same location his grandfather had shown him long ago. His grandfather had told him of his great-grandfather, a renowned warrior, fighting the white soldiers to protect his people. Because of him and other young warriors a small band of Cherokee had escaped into the Blue Ridge Mountains and not been force-marched west on the long Trail of Tears. This had been the place his great-grandfather had come to on his vision quest. This was the place where he had dreamed of the turmoil to come. This was a sacred place that called only the greatest warriors, that is how he knew Dylan would find it. She had the spirit of the Hawk within her. It had given her the strength to fight in the long battle in the desert. But the Hawk totem was now wild and fierce, out of control. It must be tempered by another totem animal and Dylan must find her totem guide for these peaceful days or the Spirit Hawk would tear her soul apart.

Gray Hawke drifted back to his lodge, like Dylan he often found comfort in the flames of the fire. As he stared into the flames he went over a plan in his head. It was crazy but it might be the only thing to save his granddaughter. He went to the room Dylan had been in the night before and searched her bag. He pulled out her cellular phone and returning to the living room he sat back in his chair and began searching the phones memory.

Having finally arrive home by cab, Nathan had called the nearest florist and had two-dozen long stem roses delivered to the Grant estate, one dozen red roses for Lura and one dozen yellow roses for Mrs. Grant.

The flowers were returned to his home, rejected, the card unopened. He sat on the kitchen floor, a glass in hand and an open bottle of Scotch on the Italian tile floor next to him.

Lura walked down the long stairs of the main foyer and turned towards the large mahogany doors that led to her father's home office. Tapping lightly, she waited for an answer.

A voice called out, "Come in Lura honey, have a seat." Opening the door quietly Lura saw her father at his desk, his head bent in concentration. One hand held a pen poised over a thick document, the other held a phone to his ear. He was apparently deeply involved in a conversation and was unwilling to break the call.

She looked around the room, curiosity and impatience making her restless. She had rarely been in this part of the house, it had become known as her father's sanctuary. Her occasional visits to this part of the house and this room, in particular, had usually been memorable either resulting in some form of restriction or reward, depending on the cause of the "summons". But that had been years ago, when she had been in school, now she was a grown woman, but the anxiety was still there. She went over the events of the last few days in her mind trying to determine the cause of this particular visit. Confused, she sat in one of the two oak and leather chairs facing the long matching oak and leather desk. Her hands were clenched in her lap as she waited patiently for her father to finish his telephone conversation.

"Yes, I understand. No, it's no problem, I will have the tickets tonight and the package will be on its way in the morning, umm, if not sooner." He chuckled "Thank you for calling." Harrison Grant hung up the phone, picked up a thick notepad and tapping the black

Mont Blanc pen in concentration. He quickly scribbled a note on a pad, read it, smiled and turned the pad over, obscuring it from Lura's view. Pushing a button on the keyboard of his phone he waited patiently for the ring to be answered.

"Yes, Sir?" came the prompt response in a very proper male voice.

"Richard, I need you to make reservations for me. One ticket, one way, Richmond to Raleigh, first class departing tomorrow, open return. Also, I will need a rental car, no make that an SUV, standing by at the airport. Do you have all that?"

"Of course, Sir," came the confident response.

"Thank you, Richard. Now hold all my calls for the next fifteen minutes." He pushed the button and disconnected. He flipped the notepad over again, finished the note, smiled and put the pen away. Finally, he lifted his head and stared at his very confused and nervous daughter.

"Hello dear," he said in a calm cool voice. Glancing back at his pad he smiled and looked again at his daughter. Clearing his throat he glanced into green eyes and let the smile slip from his face.

"Lura, it seems that you have been lax in some things. You neglected to inform me or your mother of an…umm… relationship, shall we call it? Between yourself and one Captain Dylan Hawke. What the hell is going on here, Lura? Are you seriously involved with this woman?" he asked, cool brown eyes stared deeply into hers. "What were you thinking?"

Lura sat there stunned, her mouth hanging open. *How did he find out? Well to hell with him and to hell with mother. I love Dylan and that is all there is to it.*

"Yes, Father, I am involved with her, and yes, it is serious, or at least I hope it is," she said, glancing down at her folded hands, her heart racing. *Wait, what do I have to be ashamed of?* She thought, unconsciously bringing her head up proudly.

"Well, I am not sure about this Lura," Harrison stated, rising from his chair and walking around to the front of his desk. He folded his arms and leaned back against the huge piece of furniture staring down intimidatingly at his daughter. "I am not sure that I will allow any daughter of mine to become involved in that sort of relationship. What will people think?" he asked in a deep, calm voice, his brows furrowed in concern.

Lura sat there, her head bent once again under her father's glare. As she stared at her fingers she remembered the bruises, the feel of a soft breast swelling in her hand, the gentle touch of long callused finger curled around hers. To give all that up? *For what? Appearances?*

"NO!" she screamed. Lura slammed her hands down on the arms of the chair. Her head still bowed and her eyes closed, she drew in a deep breath, raised her head again and stared at her father. "I have no intention of listening to another word, Father," she said in disgust. "I am only going to say this one time, so listen good, and memorize this because you will need to repeat it to mother for me since you will probably disown me for what I am about to say."

Lura stood slowly and stepped up to her tall father. She leaned forward as if to touch her nose to her father's. "Dylan Hawke is a wonderful, beautiful, heroic woman. She saved my life and owns my heart. I would give up everything for her, even you." By now tears were welling in her eyes, angry hurt tears. She faced her father, her jaw clenched, her eyes flashing with stubborn determination.

"You know, Father, I thought that mother would give me a hard time over this and I was ready for it, but you really surprise me. Of all the people in my life I though I could rely on you were number one on my list."

Harrison stared into those angry eyes, a frown creasing his brow. "What exactly do you mean by that Lura? You are my daughter and as long as you live under my roof..."

"What? What, Father? Are you going to kick me out, disown me, cut me from the will? Well, I really don't give a damn, do it. I will find a job, I will wait tables, I will do whatever it takes. I love you and I love mother, but Dylan is my world. God, Father." She threw up her arms in frustration. "When I am with her, I don't need anything else, or anyone else. As long as we are together, we can do anything and the only opinion that matters to me is hers. As long as she loves me..."

Lura stopped here. Did Dylan love her? Why did she leave if she truly loved her?

Harrison watched the confused look replace the anger; he had a pretty good idea where that look came from.

"Lura? Lura, I'm sorry honey. I had to find out." He turned Lura to face him and pulled his daughter into his arms and gently rubbed her back.

"What? What are you talking about? Find out what?" She drew back from her father staring into his eyes. "What kind of game are you playing, Dad?" Anger again replaced her confusion.

Harrison felt his daughter drawing back from him. He knew that the little spitfire that was his daughter was definitely getting her hackles up. He also knew that he was pushing his luck with her.

"Lura honey, I had to know that what you are feeling is true. I spoke to Dylan's grandfather today and..."

"YOU WHAT?" she screamed "Why? Why, Father? What gave you the right..."

"Lura, I didn't call him, he called me. Dylan needs you," he said, quietly staring straight into her eyes. "Honey, she needs you."

Lura looked deeply into her fathers eyes; she frowned knowing that he had never lied to her. She felt that she could trust him. "Dylan needs me? He said Dylan needs me? Why? What wrong? Is Dylan hurt; is she okay? Where is she? I have to go, I have to go now!"

Lura turned pulling from her fathers arms, her mind already racing through what she would need to pack, who she would call to take her to the airport and the cost of a ticket to...where?

She turned back to her father. "Where is she?" she asked, quietly her voice determined.

Her father stood there, his arms once again folded over his chest as he saw the look of angry determination on her face.

"Where is she, Father?" Lura stepped closer to her father. "Where is she? You can tell me and make this easy or not, but I will find her," she said, her voice cold and still.

"She is in Cherokee, North Carolina, or to be more specific, she is somewhere in the Blue Ridge Mountains of North Carolina. Your plane ticket will be here before you finished packing." He smiled, watching her face change. Her mouth open in a surprised, round 'O'. He grinned at her and she smiled back. With a wild whoop she threw her arms around his neck and placed a loud wet kiss on his cheek.

"You are the best!" she squealed, her heart thumping with excitement. Her heart skipped. "Wait, Dylan's grandfather called you? She is all right, isn't she? She isn't hurt or anything?" Lura's hands were gripping her father's in a white-knuckle hold.

"Ow, ease up there sweetheart, I write all my checks with that hand," Harrison groaned. "As far as I know she is fine. Her grandfather, what was his name...Gray Hawke, said that she had gone camping and needed you for some sort of ceremony. He said it was a native tradition and you had to be there. Now, before you ask, no, I have no idea what the hell kind of ceremony he is talking about. I just know that you have to be there."

He paused and looked deeply into green eyes. "Lura, I know that you and Dylan faced some real challenges. I have no idea how you two survived, but what I do know is that you love that woman and she loves you. You two have some kind of bond. I know that most people...hell especially our people, don't understand that, but I also know that you belong together. Sometimes, if a person is very, very lucky, if they are in the right place at just the right time something very special happens. You meet someone, someone so special that they touch something deep inside; they touch your soul. It is so rare that no one should stand between them. No one has the right to interfere with that. I see that between you and this woman, I saw it when we watched the award ceremony in Washington. I saw it when you arrived here without her and I see it now. I know your mother will have a small Hereford, but I want you to know that what ever you decide, you have my blessings. I love you, Lura." Harrison hugged his daughter close knowing that the path she had chosen would be one filled with trials. He smiled knowing that she was more than a match for any type of challenge and anything she couldn't handle, the tall, dark haired soldier could.

He had to let his little girl go.

CHAPTER 10

Alison Grant was not one to listen at keyholes but she had to think of the family's reputation, even if Harrison didn't. She walked down the hall away from Harrison's office to a much smaller room. A young man sat behind a cherry wood desk dialing numbers and taking notes.

"Richard, there has been a slight delay in plans, Miss Lura is not leaving until Monday. I need you to reschedule things for then. I am throwing her a surprise going away party so this will be our little secret, okay?" Alison said smiling at the young man.

"Umm, I'm sorry Mrs. Grant, but I take my orders from Mr. Grant. I would need his permission to make those changes," Richard stated, glancing up at Mrs. Grant. He knew that Harrison Grant would have a large piece of his rear if he ignored or changed any direct requests and Alison was known to become "involved" in the company business where her personal needs were concerned. He wasn't sure what was going on but unless he got a call from Mr. Grant he was not changing anything.

Alison was furious, how dare that young nobody tell her no? When she finished dealing with Lura's little problem she would see to it that he was informed of his station. She turned on her heel and huffed out the room. There was more than one way to fix this problem. Mrs. Grant climbed the stairs to the second floor and strolled down the hall to her private salon, pushing the door open, she smiled at the beautiful bright room. She had decorated this room herself and it was her retreat when things got too stressful in the real world. The entire room was done in shades of white, cream and gold. The delicate French provincial furniture was actually Louis XV and had cost Harrison a small fortune but, she smiled, *I am worth it after all.*

Alison walked over and sat behind the delicate cream desk and picked up the hand set of the antique phone, the old fashioned rotary dial face was very beautiful but tended to rub the polish on her nails. She reached into the desk drawer and pulled out a dialing stick. Placing the rounded head in the finger holes she dialed the airport.

Yes, there is more than one way to fix this little problem.

The phone was answered on the third ring, Alison spoke softly into the receiver, "Hello, this is Lura Grant. My father's secretary just called to make reservations for me and something has come up. I need to change my flight..."

Lura was floating on cloud nine. She didn't need to worry about anything now except finding her Hawk. Her father knew all about them and he didn't care, he just wanted her to be happy. She raced up the stairs and into her room where she opened the closet door and began throwing clothes onto her bed. Jeans, sweaters, long sleeved sweatshirts and lightweight jackets, all joined the pile. Next she bent to sort through her shoes, hiking shoes and sneakers joined the growing assortment of clothing. The boots and sneakers kept disappearing only to reappear in the trash, so she had hidden them in the back of her closet until she needed them.

Smiling and humming to herself, Lura went to her second closet and pulled out her suitcase. She reached in again and came out with a large backpack and placing both on the bed she began packing, her mind already in flight and heading south.

Alison hung up the phone, it had been difficult to make all the changes but she had been successful. Now she had two days to work on changing her daughter's mind, two short days to keep her daughter from ruining her life and Alison's reputation and social standing. She needed to find someone to help her and as much as she detested Nathan, he was the only one available on such short notice. With a groan and a sigh she went back to the phone and began dialing again.

Nathan had finished the first bottle of Scotch and unfortunately, he was still conscious. He reached up and grabbed the counter, pulling himself to his feet just as the kitchen phone rang.

"Nathan Owen the third," he answered with a drunken slur.

"Nathan, this is Alison Grant," responded the cultured voice on the other end of the line.

"You sound strange. Are you alright?" Alison asked concern in her tone.

"Yes, yes I'm fine. I was lounging in the library over a good book and I fell asleep." The lie slipped smoothly from his lips. "I guess I shouldn't have played that last round of golf at the club this afternoon," Nathan said, now sweating into the phone.

"Umm, yes of course," Alison responded, not believing a word he said. Lura was right, he was slime but she would use him long enough to get Lura straightened out and then she would find someone more suitable for her son-in-law.

"Nathan, Lura is going away for a few days and her father and I are throwing her a surprise party. A few hundred people, just a small gathering of family and close friends. We would like you to attend. Are you free on Saturday?"

Nathan felt his heart leap, "Yes, of course…what time?" He winced at the eager tone evident to his own ears.

Gotcha! Alison smiled, *if all goes well, Lura will realize how unacceptable and foolish her little crush is and I can make her see what a waste she is making of her life. Nathan is an idiot but he is male and that is all I need, for now.*

"Cocktails will be served at six o'clock, this is a casual affair so a sports coat is acceptable. I will see you then, and Nathan, no more childish antics! Understand?" She hung up before he could answer.

Nathan stared at the phone. *What just happened* he thought? *Who cares, I have a second chance and I'm not about to screw this up again.* Dollar signs flashed through his brain and he rushed upstairs to look for a clean sports coat and slacks.

Harrison was tired of waiting. For some reason Richard had not answered his page nor responded to his calls. He slid back from his desk and standing, walked to the door. Pulling the heavy door open he scowled down the hall in the direction of his secretary's office. Richard was pacing back and forth across the hall mumbling to himself and scanning several sheets of paper. Though his secretary was a bit unusual and a perfectionist to the point of being anal retentive, Harrison knew this was unusual behavior even for Richard.

"Richard!" he bellowed, "Why haven't you answered your phone? Didn't you hear me calling?"

"Yes, Sir," the quiet young man responded. "I supposed that you were calling to check on the reservations. I…I…I"

"Oh for the love of God man, spit it out," Harrison said frustrated with the babbling.

"Well, I am not sure what to say, sir. I called and made all the reservations just as you requested. But when I went to print them out the dates…well, see for yourself." He handed the stack of white pages to the silver haired Harrison. Harrison scanned the documents, his expression becoming more clouded with each line.

"I told you specifically to schedule the flight for tomorrow, not Saturday. Can't you follow simple instructions?"

"Why, yes sir, I can," the young man responded. "I checked the reservations twice but when I called the airlines again, they told me that Ms. Grant called and changed them, Ms. Lura Grant."

"But Lura wouldn't…wait. I bet…no, she wouldn't…yes, she would. Bitch!" Harrison was furious. He crumbled the pages in his hand as he turned and headed towards the stairs. "She has controlled that girl long enough, she is not going to ruin this for her. I will not stand for it." He took the stairs two at a time, his anger at the boiling point. Striding down the hall he threw open Alison's salon door.

"Alison! I know you are in here. Alison!" he called. His lovely wife strolled into the salon and up to him, placing a quick peck on his cheek.

"Yes dear? I really wish you would not bellow so, what would the neighbors think?" She smiled, straightening his tie.

"To hell with the neighbors!" Harrison continued. "Why did you change Lura's reservations? And don't even try to deny it, Lura would have never changed them," he growled.

"Well, dear, when I accidentally overheard you asking Richard to make plane reservations for Lura, I was just torn. I just got my dear daughter back and here you were sending her off to some wild country again. Well, I just had to give her a going away party; it is only fair, dear. Who knows when she will be back? After all, you made it a one-way flight. I just couldn't let my little girl go without a proper farewell. She can still go, I just moved the date back a few days. Is it too much to ask to allow a mother to say goodbye to her child?" She pouted looking up at Harrison with the same hazel/green eyes as his daughter.

He knew he was beaten and Harrison felt his shoulders slump in defeat. *What in the world will I tell Lura* he thought as he walked from the room, his wife at his heels.

CHAPTER 11

With her pack securely on her back and her small suitcase in hand, Lura trotted down the stairs, a smile on her lips. She had to call the driver and have him come around for the bags. Her heart danced as she thought of the look on Dylan's face when she opened her front door.

"Humm, I wonder if I have enough time to make a quick stop at the mall," she mumbled aloud to herself. Adjusting the straps on the backpack she carefully placed it at the door next to her suitcase. She reached up and patted her cheeks. The muscles were taxed and a bit sore from smiling, but she could not help herself, the smile just wouldn't go away. Her mind kept returning to the image of a beautiful woman in black, a small isolated cave and a warm golden fire.

Spinning on her heel she strolled back to her father's office to call the driver and pick up her tickets. She tapped softly on the heavy door and waited. A deep voice called her into the room and she pushed the door open and stepped in. Looking around the room she was surprised to see her father's secretary and her mother standing with her father in front of his desk. Alarms began to go off when she noticed the smug look of success on her mother's face and the look of anger in her father's eyes.

"Um, Dad? What's going on? Is everything

okay?" she asked. Her question addressed to her father, but her eyes were on her mother's smiling face.

"No Lura, everything is not okay. Your mother has taken it upon herself to cancel your reservations," he said in an angry heated tone. "She has rescheduled your flight for Monday. Seems she wants to throw you a bon voyage party."

"I...I...wait! She WHAT? Mother? Please, tell me you didn't. Tell me that my flight wasn't cancelled." Lura looked at her mother with pleading eyes.

Alison Grant simply smiled and then glanced at her watch. "Well, I am sorry dear, but the last flight out to Atlanta leaves at six thirty and believe me, it is sold out. Now, we have some planning to do. You have to get your hair done and we simply must buy you a new dress. You have nothing to wear to a party," Alison stated, ignoring the stunned look on her daughters face.

"Like HELL I will mother! You just don't get it, do you? I am leaving and I am leaving today. I don't give a damn if it is by plane, train or automobile. I am out of here. I will not be attending any stupid party, I am going to find the woman I love and if you can't understand that then to hell with you, Mother."

Lura turned to her father. "Dad, can I borrow the car?" Harrison Grant grinned at his daughter and reached into his pocket.

"Take the Benz, the tank is full and my gas card is in the glove box. Bring that soldier girl of yours home when you find her. I would love to meet her," he said tossing the keys to Lura.

Lura snatched the keys out of the air and rushed to her father. She threw her arms around his neck, placing a loud wet kiss on his cheek. "You are the best, you know that? I love you, Dad."

With a final hug she turned and rushed from the room. Flying up the stairs she threw open the doors to her suite and rushed in. Had there been a fly on the wall it would have smiled watching the young woman rush madly around the room talking to herself.

"I've got one important stop to make before I hit the road and if I am going to make it to Gray Hawk's anytime soon, I had better get rolling."

Adding a few last minute items she zipped her bag closed grabbed her backpack and raced down the stairs. Turning right at the bottom of the landing she ran through the formal dining room and into the kitchen. Lennie stood in the middle of the kitchen with a brown bag in hand. Her tear-streaked face was creased with a smile.

"I packed you a bag darlin'. Now you be careful on the road and don't you dare talk to any strangers. Oh, and give that cute soldier of yours a kiss for this old woman will ya?" she said smiling as she hugged Lura. Lura could only grin and nod in response as she ran from the room.

Outside she headed for the garage, but noticed that her father had asked the driver to pull the Benz around front. She redirected her flying feet in that direction. Reaching the vehicle she opened the back door and threw her luggage across the seat. Slamming the door she snatched the front door handle, hoisted herself up on the running boards and slid into the front seat.

She cranked up the Benz and revved the engine, enjoying the powerful purr of the SUV. Stomping on the gas pedal she waved and grinned as she heard the sound of gravel fly.

"Why Harrison? Do you know what this is going to do to our reputation? What will people say when they find out our daughter is a...a, my God, I can't even bring myself to say it. A lesbian?" Alison whispered. "How could you? You are going to condone this? You are going to subject us to the ridicule of our friends? Why? Just give me one good reason why?"

"For love, Alison, something you obviously have forgotten about," Harrison stated coldly. He moved around his desk to stare out the large lead glass windows onto the front lawn. He was happy as he watched his daughter open the doors of the Mercedes ML55 SUV, toss the bag and backpack into the back seat and grabbing the front to open the driver's door. She pulled herself up onto the running boards and into the front seat. With a smile and a wave to her father she started the engine, revved it up and squealed down the drive, her blond head barely visible over the plush leather headrest.

Alison Grant watched as her daughter disappeared down the long drive and out of the main gate. *This just can't be happening. All my planning, all my hard work to establish myself as a leader in the community. All wasted, out the window. Why and for what? An inappropriate affair with a strange woman, if she wanted to have an affair, she should do something more socially acceptable and go to Europe for her sordid flings. What will people think?*

Alison bit her well-manicured nail as she walked

from the room. Hurrying back up the stairs, she entered her private salon and sat at her desk to think. Suddenly a thought occurred to her. She picked up her address book again, looked up the name and dialed the number. A few minutes later she hung up, confident that all would be well. Gloating, she dialed a second number and scheduled herself for a massage and manicure.

Lura pulled into the first rest stop on I-95, her mind took her back to her last visit here and she scowled. Reaching into her black CD case she pulled out her worn copy of SKIN and slipped it into the player. The Alpine hummed and surrounded her with the sultry tones of Melissa. She closed her eyes and relaxed back into the soft leather of the seat, her mind picturing her soldier in blue.

He watched the blond first smile then lay back in the driver's seat. She was listening to music and napping, so tempting but he would wait. There was plenty of time...now.

The air was fresh and crisp, the scent of pine mixing with the smell of cedar. The morning was chilly and brisk. It was the kind of day she had grown up with and she smiled remembering the mornings with the young men of the village. She had spent one wonderful summer camping with her grandfather and other young would be warriors as the old War Chief taught them the ways of the Cherokee. Those skills had come in handy later when she had become a silent deadly killer.

The smile faded from her face as new memories replaced the old. Quietly Dylan rolled out of her shelter and began her day. No use staying abed with the thoughts that haunted her, this was the day that would begin the cleansing.

Dylan quickly and efficiently gathered kindling and firewood, cedar, pine and oak. Going to her shelter she reached into her pack and found a lighter and beginning with the pine she built a fire pit and started the flames. The pine and cedar would produce a great deal of cleansing smoke and the cedar would evoke the spirits and take her prayers to the old ones, the spirits of the great and wise warriors of the past.

She stood and turned back to the edge of the clearing. She had found a small stream the previous night and had enjoyed fresh trout for dinner. Now she would wash herself in preparation of the quest.

Stripping naked, she left her clothing in the shelter and continued to the stream. The mountain water was like ice and goose bumps sprang up on her skin. Using the white sand at the bottom of the stream, she scrubbed her arms and legs, her feet and hands, her breasts and belly. Finally she rinsed. The finely powdered sand mixed with the icy water left her skin rosy and tingling. Stepping from the stream she walked, dripping from the icy water, to stand before the fire. The smoke, now full, wrapped around her body like a soft cloak, while the flames slowly, gently dried her chilled skin and warmed her. She thought of the last three years in the desert. She tried to remember each day, each night and each man she had killed. She remembered the burning hatred she had felt and the desire for vengeance that had eaten away at her soul.

Finally dry, she pulled a burning cedar limb from the flames and followed the path she had laid the day before into the sweat lodge. Once inside she touched the cedar to the wood in the fire pit and began the slow lengthy chant to invoke the totem spirits.

Lura woke to the rolling sound of wheels as another SUV passed behind her, the sound of tires on gravel causing her to start. Alarmed and disoriented she sat up quickly and looked around, she had fallen asleep in the car. She glanced at her face in the mirror, thinking that it was the best sleep she'd had since she returned home. Checking the gas gauge she sat the back of the seat up straight and tightened her seat belt. Shifting the car into reverse she slowly backed up and headed for the merge ramp onto I-95.

She didn't notice the dark shadow trailing her car as she pulled into the flow of traffic; her mind was hours and miles away. She cranked up the music, rolled down all the windows and opened the sunroof. Reaching into her backpack she pulled out her favorite baseball cap and slipped it on her head, pulling her hair through the opening in the back to keep it out of her face. Reaching into the glove box she fumbled around until she found a pair of Ray Bans, her father's, and slid them on as she pressed the gas.

The dark shadow accelerated to keep up, the driver smiling as he watched the SUV pull into traffic totally oblivious of the fact that he had cut a tiny hole in her tire while she slept.

Lura tapped the steering wheel to the sultry beat of Melissa Manchester as she checked the rear view mirrors, flipped on her indicator and eased into the fast lane.

Oh yeah, put that hammer down girl, she thought

as she accelerated past the small four door sedan that was slowing her down.

She had lost a bit of time falling asleep in the rest stop but with any luck she could make it up by driving straight through to the state line before she stopped again.

As she pulled into the left lane she felt the outside rear tire bump. She checked the rear view again but didn't see anything that may have caused the thumping noise. She continued driving but turned off the music so she could concentrate on the sounds of the car. She felt the thumping again and realized that the rear tire was losing air. Slowing she turned on her hazard blinkers and looked for an exit.

Behind her the driver in the dark sedan smirked. *Soon,* he thought, *real soon Lura Grant.* Grinning he followed the disabled vehicle.

Lura kept her eyes on the road signs hoping to see a service station sign for the next exit. She also kept an eye on traffic behind her as she limped along noticing that no one seemed inclined to assist her. Several people honked as they passed gesturing their frustrations as they flew by. Initially Lura simple ignored them and frowned as the irritated travelers passed, but after the fifth car whizzed by honking and gesturing, Lura had endured all she could take. She had just taken a deep breath and begun to wind up and let fly when she saw blue lights blinking in her rear view mirror.

"Now what? As if I didn't have enough trouble..." Lura eased the car to the shoulder and pulled her backpack to the front seat. She turned the engine off and began searching for her driver's license and insurance card.

A tap sounded on her window and she lowered it to speak. A pretty young trooper stood at the window.

"Ma'am, seems you have a bad tire," she said smiling.

"Humm, what gave it away?" Lura smiled, chuckling with relief to see another woman as she passed her the license and registration. The trooper laughed and glanced down at the license.

"Okay Ms Grant, tell ya what. You follow me to the next off ramp. There is a service station there and I know the mechanic." She tipped her hat and handed Lura back her identification. That was when Lura noticed the ring on her finger. The stones were rainbow colored.

Family! Lura grinned as she cranked up the truck and slid in behind the trooper car.

Damn, damn, damn he thought as he pounded on the steering column. He had her then that damn stupid trooper had to show up. *That's okay, there will be another chance.* He pulled back into traffic and eased by the trooper's sedan and the SUV.

Dylan poked at the fire adding more limbs to the blaze. The heat was intense and she was sweating rivers. She wiped the salt from her eyes and lay back on the soft blanket that covered her bed of pine straw. Closing her eyes she worked on bringing to mind the events of the last three years. She hung them out on the smoke and heat and reviewed each event as if seeing it through the unbiased eyes of a stranger.

She watched the attack on her unit and the death of her men. She watched herself stagger through the sand to fall unconscious by the cool waters of the oasis. She saw the faces of the desert people who had taken her in and healed her; she saw the fear in their eyes when they realized what they had brought into their homes.

These thoughts saddened her because she did not want to see the fear on the faces of those gentle people. It tore at her heart.

Ashamed, she cried silently, her tears mixing with the sweat as it rolled from her eyes to soak into her hair. She kept on, her mind taking her on a path, a vision quest of her life. She saw the faces of the enemy, the men she had killed, but this time she was an observer. She saw them attack the helpless villagers, killing the men and then raping woman and young girls. She watched as a dark figure in black came out of the night and defended the helpless villagers. She saw her face twisted in pain and anger as she fired again and again until her weapon was empty only to fight on bare handed to drive off the attackers.

Now she saw that she had saved lives by fighting, that she had stopped the death of many people and she had been able to prevent families from being destroyed. She watched as a young blond boarded a plane, her face alive with the excitement of facing a new adventure.

Smiling, Dylan watched Lura elbow the man next to her who seemed determined to turn the young woman into his own personal lounge pillow. She saw the frustration on the face of a reporter hungry for a story but stopped at every angle and sent on wild goose chases through the streets of foreign towns searching for a shadow called Hawk.

Her heart leapt in her throat as she saw the van Lura traveled in forced off the road and the young reporter roughly tossed into an ancient SUV driven by the terrorist. She watched Lura fight the men who had come to rape her, then the rescue from the tent when she had taken the beaten woman into the night.

When she her mind drift on to thoughts of Lura, she saw in her vision a huge hawk. Its talons were sharp and its beak open as if in a silent cry. The hawk was angry, its hackles rose as it cried over and over again. The golden wings of the hawk spread and beat the air as it fought an unseen enemy.

A large wolf loped out of the mist of her dream and sat watching the hawk. The wolf was huge, a silver and black beast with blue-white eyes. It sat with its tongue lolled out almost smiling as it watched the hawk struggle. There was a disturbance in the air and Dylan was amazed to see a graceful falcon drop from the sky. Reaching out with sharp beak and talons the falcon dove through the invisible enemy that fought the hawk. The hawk rolled away, struggling to reach a misty precipice. Screaming in victory, the falcon folded its wings and came to rest next to the hawk. Once the falcon landed the hawk settled and began to preen the smaller bird. The delicate falcon nestled closer to the large hawk never fearing that the larger bird would turn on it.

She watched, as the two seemed to melt together, each content in the presence of the other.

Still stunned, Dylan was amazed when the wolf turned its beautiful sleek head and seemed to stare through the smoke and mist directly at her.

Startled from her dream she sat up shivering, as

she heard the howl of a wolf in the distance. *Funny, there haven't been any wolves in the Carolina mountains for at least 50 years.* Dylan thought.

Lura, watched as the new tire was put on the rim of the Benz. The state trooper was in her car calling in a report. It seemed someone has slashed the tire just deep enough to allow the air to slowly leak out. Jessica, the state trooper, had been very concerned. Lura knew that her father had just gotten the truck back from the dealership where it had been in for its 15,000-mile service and everything that could be done had been done. She pulled out her mobile phone and dialed then waited for the response at the other end.

"Hi Dad. No, I'm in Petersburg. I had to stop, because of a flat tire," she told him. She held the phone away from her ear and listened as her father turned the air blue with his opinion of Mercedes Benz mechanics. When he finally stopped to take a breath she told him that the mechanics had not been at fault rather that the tire had been slashed. She held the phone away from her ear again as the voice on the other end grew louder.

The state trooper had stepped out of her car and stood grinning as she too heard the lengthy, loud string of curses coming from the phone.

"Your Dad?" she asked.

"Umm, yep, that would be him," Lura commented, scratching her cheek in embarrassment as the trooper broke into rolling laughter.

"Who is there Lura? Who's laughing in the background?" Harrison asked.

"Oh, sorry Dad, that was the State Trooper who escorted me off the highway. She was really nice about it, she even helped me find a mechanic."

Lura did not mention that the mechanic was a tall, leggy redhead who just happened to be the trooper's partner. She watched as the mechanic drove the SUV to the edge of the parking lot, wiped her hands on a towel and tossed her the keys with a roguish wink.

"Well, you make sure you get her name Lura so I can send a letter to her supervisor," Harrison stated. "Gotta take care of anyone who helps my girl."

She could hear the smile on the other end of the phone.

"Now, tell me more about this tire. When did it happen, who was around and are you okay?"

"Whoa, Dad, slow down a bit. All I can tell you is that I stopped at the last rest stop and fell asleep. It must have happened then. Probably just someone playing a mean trick. I'm okay and I plan on gassing up then I'm not stopping until I get to Gray Hawk's place."

"Good girl, you call me when you get there and don't forget to grab something to eat." There was a long pause and then Harrison's voice came over the line. "I love you, Lura."

She was touched hearing the crack in his voice. "I love you too, Daddy. Talk to you soon."

She pressed disconnect and ended the call. Slipping her cell phone back into her pack she turned and smiled as she watched the state trooper quickly and shyly hug her partner then place her hat on her head seemingly donning the "I'm a tough trooper" attitude at the same time.

The mechanic stood back and grinned shaking her head as her trooper turned and headed towards Lura. Still smiling Lura waved a thank you to the mechanic and, like the trooper, slid into the driver seat and cranked up the car.

CHAPTER 12

Dylan had been in the sweat hut now for two days. The heat inside the small shelter was intense but compared to what she had endured over the last three years, quite bearable. No it wasn't the heat that affected her, it was the water and food or the lack of both. She should have felt the thirst; felt the hunger in her belly that should have felt like a tightening in her stomach.

But Dylan was not aware of thirst or her hunger. She was deep in sleep, held there by her vision, by the guide that had come to lead her through the challenges of her quest.

Dylan followed the footprints in the ashes and the sand. She walked again the path she had made over the past three years.

More times than she wanted to see, the path was slippery and wet with blood. It was the blood of her soldiers, the blood of the enemy, but many times it was her own blood. She saw the face of the Hawk twisted in anger and hate when she fought the terrorist.

The Dylan in her vision was quick, agile and often seemed fearless, she stepped uncaring into the heat of battle often facing seemingly overwhelming

126

odds. This Hawk had no other will but to fight and destroy the enemy, her eyes were only alive when they were facing the challenge of combat. Dylan witnessed this she watched her past like a stranger watching a horror movie. She felt her spirit crumble in pain as the Hawk killed over and over again. Tears filled her eyes and she hung her head in shame.

Surprisingly, she felt her hand warmed. Glancing down she found it buried in a gray and silver pelt. She stroked the coarse hair, following her hand forward to look into the white eyes of a huge wolf. She should have felt fear; instead she felt peace. She had hated the Hawk of her vision but she watched through the eyes of the wolf and saw the truth. The fierce Hawk had been needed to meet and survive the time of the desert. Now Dylan needed to understand that the Hawk of the desert was not evil, simply a survivor.

She cried, her tears leaving salty trails down her cheeks.

The wolf nudged her hand, but she could not bring herself to move, the wolf leaned heavily against her leg and she felt herself stagger forward past the blood and death.

She watched her arms encircle a small figure, her heart beat faster as she watched them embrace, their bodies glowing in the firelight as they made love through the night.

She felt a heat, but it was not the fire, that was too cold. Nor was it the heat of the stones that was an icy heat. This was warmth that began deep inside and radiated through her body. She felt it creep into her bones, tingling through her skin and peaking in the smile on her lips. She knew the cause of the heat and she was not surprised to hear the cry of a falcon.

Glancing down again, she absentmindedly buried her hand in the wolf's mane and smiled.

Lura drove on through the night pushing herself. The traffic on Interstate 95 and Interstate 85 had not been bad and until her unexpected delay in Petersburg, she had been making good time.

As she merged from Interstate 85 South she began to tire. The next two legs of the journey she knew were going to be the hardest, first with I-85 then onto to I-40. Usually she just drove until she was bored or tired then checked into a roadside hotel for the night. But now her concern was to get to Dylan as quickly as possible so late night layovers were out of the question.

The hum of her tires on the road was mesmerizing; the flashes of the white dashes dividing the lanes caused a hypnotizing effect. All this, combined with the fact that she was already exhausted, forced the young woman to take refuge in the next rest stop.

Pulling in, Lura parked the SUV under a brilliant streetlight in front of the main building. She turned off the music, closed the windows, turned the air down and reclined the driver's seat.

"Fifteen minutes, I only need fifteen minutes," she mumbled to herself. Closing her eyes she quickly drifted off.

On the far side of the parking area a car door opened, a figure emerged and first entered the building heading towards the restrooms. The parking lot was nearly empty except for the solitary sedan, now empty, and the quiet rumble of the Mercedes SUV engine. The figure paused on his trek towards the rest rooms. He turned and glanced back at the SUV. With a nod he slowly walked toward the vehicle.

Lura was fast asleep, her mind on visions of Dylan hurt and calling to her. Why else would Gray Hawk send for her?

As Lura nodded off the figure slowly approached the truck, he peeked into the rear window then walked around to the driver's door. He paused to look inside and noticed the sleeping woman. Reaching into his pocket he drew out a set of keys and tapped on the glass. The noise startled Lura and she quickly sat up her nerves already on edge. She stared up into the face of a stranger, her eyes wide with fear.

"Sorry to startle you," the young man said. "Do you have any change? The coffee machine only takes quarters and the change machine seems to be empty."

Lura did not open the window, but simply stared at the young man then shook her head. The man waved his thanks then headed back towards the restrooms. Lura pressed the recline switch on the driver's seat, raised it and then she put the truck in reverse and left the rest stop. She was definitely wide-awake now.

Dylan felt as if she were swimming through mud, trying to reach the surface. She felt a grip on her ankle and looked back to see the wolf gently restraining her. There was more she needed to see. She nodded her head and turned back to the path. Her feet now rested on strange soft brown earth, new grass just beginning to peek between her toes. She felt refreshed; the feeling of dread had lifted from her shoulders. But there was something that still troubled her. She watched as an image slowly materialized, the setting was familiar, the voices were angry. It was her parents, but they looked different, younger.

Dylan watched as her father paced in the living room of their old home. His arms were flailing the air while his angry voice was directed at her mother. She remembered this argument, it had occurred the night of her eighteenth birthday. She had not been able to hear the entire conversation; she had been confined to quarters, her room. That was the night she had packed her bags and left.

Her mother was crying, unable to stop her fathers ranting. Her grandfather had stood there silent until the younger man had finished.

Finally Gray Hawk spoke. "You young pup!" he said in a cold hard voice. "That is your daughter that you were speaking of. She is the flesh of your flesh. You should feel greatly honored to have one such as she, touched by the Great Spirit. In the old days she would be revered and trained to be a great warrior. Yet you do not see in her the promise of greatness, you only see something that is not of your kind, something different than others. You see this as a blemish on your career. But she is no blemish, she is simply your daughter." The old man folded his arms over his chest and stared at the young version of her father.

Dylan was stunned to see tears in her father's eyes. He hung his head in shame

"God, what was I thinking?" he whispered. Going

to a chair in the living room he collapsed, his head in his hands.

Gray Hawk watched, his eyes cold at first, then warming. He walked over and knelt beside her father.

"You must go and speak to your daughter. She is deeply wounded by your angry words."

"I will." He stood and walked down the hall, noticing that no light was coming under the door to Dylan's room. Turning he walked back to the living room.

"She's asleep, I will speak to her in the morning. Maybe we can talk and she can explain why. I will try to understand," he said, his head down and his shoulders slumped.

The scene faded and Dylan continued on. As she watched a second scene began to unfold, it was her old bedroom; she smiled seeing items from her past.

"God, was I always that junky?" she questioned herself, amazed at the magnitude of clutter she saw thrown about her room. She watched as the door opened and her parents walked in.

"Dylan? Dylan honey?" her mother called. Her father walked around the room staring at first one thing then another, slowly the truth surfacing on his face.

"She isn't here, she's run away. Our little girl has run away." Dylan watched as her mother sat down on the edge of her bed with a stunned look on her face.

"Why? Where could she go?" her mother asked in a choked voice.

"It's my fault, I should never have spoken to her like that," he said. "Don't worry, honey. I will find her; I will find our little girl and bring her home. I promise," the Senator stated as he sat next to his wife and pulled her into his arms.

Dylan was stunned. He had wanted to apologize all those years ago. Had she not run away...

She shook her head in anger; she had only been a young girl. He should have tried to understand, not attack her like he did. No, she had done the right thing.

Dylan turned her back to the scene and began walking in a different direction. As she walked on, a new image began to appear. It was her father again; he sat in his huge office in Washington. It was late in the evening; the outer offices were dark, evidence that he was working late and alone.

"Humph, he should be home with mother and not constantly working. Doesn't he know that she needs him?"

Then a second thought sprang into her mind. *She wouldn't be alone if you had not run away.*

The voice was not her own, definitely female, but very rough. Startled, she glanced down and met the eerie blue eyes of the wolf. The look in the wolf's eyes told Dylan that the voice had, somehow, come from the wolf.

Shaking her head she walked around the desk to stand behind her father, reading over his shoulder. She was stunned to see her father reviewing her military records.

What right does he have? She asked herself, angry to see this man studying the records of the last few years of her life.

The rights of a father who is concerned for his child, the voice said. Dylan did not bother looking down; she recognized the voice of the wolf.

We have to go on. There is more to show you, the wolf said.

Dylan turned and walked from the image of her father's office, still angry over the last vision.

This was all so strange. She glanced down to see her naked feet treading on clouds; they moved with her and swirled around her. The whole world was a soft lavender blue; it was all beautiful and very tranquil.

She hated it!

Grumbling under her breath, Dylan followed the wolf glancing around wishing for a stone or a stick or even a lumpy cloud to kick. Why was her spirit guide showing her these images?

Because you need to see them, you need to see the truth.

"Damn it! Get the Hell out of my head!" Dylan exclaimed, thumping the side of her head with the butt of her hand.

"I have enough problems with my mind speaking to me. I really don't need some crazy canine running around in there too," she said scowling down at the wolf.

Stop being a cub and pay attention. The wolf replied, ignoring the scowling naked woman at her side.

Dylan wanted to tell the wolf to go to hell, but for all she knew, that was exactly where they were, purple clouds or no purple clouds. Still grumbling, she followed the wolf.

The new scene in front of her was a familiar one. She had spent many days here studying the books about tracking and survival in the hope that her grandfather would one day give in and allow her to go on the summer trips that the young men took each year. The library had always felt like a warm place, safe and comfortable. It was not a large library by any stretch of the imagination, but it was well stocked.

She looked around seeing the outdated computers, the ancient tables scattered about with students of all ages leaning over pads and books, hands gripping pencils and brows furrowed in concentration. She smiled remembering the days she had spent here trying to commit to memory all the possible skills she could find, just in case…

Well, I guess all that studying did come in handy, she mused.

Walking on, she passed walls of shelves lined with books. The library was quiet as usual. The librarian and Dylan's first crush, Miss Karen, stood behind the tall desk, her large brown eyes scanning a microfiche of titles and authors. She was just as beautiful as she had been all those years ago with long glossy black hair and beautiful creamy skin.

She stood for a moment remembering the time she first saw the cute librarian and the realization that she was attracted to her. At first she was embarrassed, not understanding her feelings. She spent hours lingering in the library just so she could watch her. She had always secretly hoped that Miss Karen would notice her and she smiled remembering the shattered heart of that young girl when Miss Karen became Mrs. Brayboy. She stayed out of the library for almost two weeks, but eventually she returned and was surprised to get a welcome back hug from Mrs. Brayboy.

Smiling she glanced around wondering why the wolf had brought her to this location, then she saw him. Her father was sitting alone at a table piled high with reference books. Mrs. Brayboy came to him with a slip of paper. She quietly laid it on his table. She stared down at her father's bent head waiting patiently for him to look up. Finally he did,

"You know, Dylan has always been a sweet, bright child. I guessed that she might be gay when she would follow me around the library. I felt flattered; she is such a wonderful little thing. I have no idea why she would run away, but I hope that whatever caused her to leave gets resolved quickly. She has a lot of friends here that are going to miss her and will probably be very upset to learn that she has run away."

With that, and a withering cold look, her sweet librarian turned her back on Dylan's father and stalked off. He watched her until she sat back down, flipped her hair out of her eyes and glared at him. With a shake of his head he returned to his study.

Dylan chuckled, watching her father's shoulders, first stiffen then slump. Her smile disappeared as she watched him drop his head into his hands, close his eyes and sigh deeply. What was he studying so diligently?

She slipped up behind him and glanced over his shoulders, forgetting that there was no need for stealth. She stared down at the title of the book, "Homosexuality, facts and fiction." Her eyes widened in disbelief as she shot a glance over at the stacks of books on the table, each one covering a single subject matter, homosexuality.

Dylan stared at the stacks of research books. *He must have every book on homosexuality in the library*, she mused. *Why?* She was angry.

"Did he think that it was a disease, that it was

catching, maybe he is looking for a cure?" she mumbled aloud.

She was startled to feel the nip of teeth in her butt and with a yelp she stared down indignantly at the wolf.

You, young one, need to learn patience, came the sound of an overly tolerant, very female voice. *Watch and learn, perhaps you may discover things that you were not aware of,* the voice continued.

Dylan stared at the wolf, the voice in her head still startling.

"Okay, okay, I'll watch but I doubt anything he does will surprise me."

There was no reply from the wolf, just a look of irritation, if you could call it that.

"Do wolves get attitudes?" Dylan asked herself.

"YES!" came the strong reply in her head.

She glanced down again surprised at the wolf who seemed to be ignoring her, much to Dylan's annoyance.

She stepped away from the wolf and wandered over towards a table thinking to sit on it and wait patiently, but reconsidered when she realized that she might simply slip through the furniture. Instead she stood crossing her arms over her naked chest in an effort to appear bored.

She watched the man she knew as her father, as he flipped from page to page, book to book, reading, taking notes and finally slowly a look of realization appeared on his face. Tears began to creep down his cheeks. He let them fall, wetting the pages of the text below.

Dylan stepped forward and read the passage that had caused the tears. It was an article about child abandonment and children who had run away. It covered topics about neglect, abuse and ... rejection.

"My God. What have I done?" the whisper came in a broken voice filled with pain and self-disgust.

Dylan watched as he slowly closed the book and wiped his face. The man that stood from that table was an older man. Exhaustion was etched on his face and in his walk. He selected one book and waited in the check out line quietly. When he laid the large book on the table Mrs. Brayboy smiled at him.

"So now you understand. Well, what are you going to do about it? Are you going to sit back on your wide political ass and disown your daughter or are you going to go look for her. If you find her you had better hope that she can still find a place in her heart for you. That little girl spent half her life looking for a father and what she got was a pig headed bigoted greedy politician. Life is short, do you think it is worth going through without your little girl?"

John Cameron stared at the small woman with the beautiful eyes. His expression began to change from hopeless to hopeful.

"Now, a little birdie told me that a young girl just got recruited for the Army not a week ago. Seems her name was Hawke, Dylan Hawke."

Dylan was shocked. Of all the people to betray her, she never expected it to be Mrs. Brayboy. She felt the nip on her butt again and looked down into the angry eyes of the wolf.

"Betray you? What makes you think she is betraying you? Remember you were only an eighteen-year-old child then. What did you think of the eighteen-year-old warriors in your unit?" the voice asked.

"Humph, they couldn't pour pee out of a boot with directions on the heel," Dylan chuckled. They needed someone to hold their hands when they crossed the street.

Well, what made you so special then, warrior? Did you not feel responsible for those young lives? Did you not feel the need to protect and safeguard them? the wolf questioned, the pale eyes narrowing on Dylan's face.

"Well, that was different. I was mature for my age," came the sulky reply.

Even she did not believe that. She scuffed a bare toe on the cloud below her feet seeing the scene before her with different eyes.

"I was not thinking," she admitted finally.

Yes, but neither was he. Perhaps you know now where you get your temper? The voice asked as the wolf and the warrior turned to watch the man leave the building.

"I know I have the right town," Lura mused flicking from low beams to high in an effort to see any street names.

"Why the hell do people even bother to name a damn street if they aren't going to put up damn street signs so you can figure out where the Hell you are, DAMN IT!" she exclaimed, feeling much better for being able to voice her opinion.

Suddenly, a large bird flew out of the bush and across her windshield.

"What the…" she yelled as she swerved sharply to the left and slammed on the brakes. The truck came to a sudden stop directly across from an unlit narrow street.

"Well, one road seems to be as good as another," she said shrugging off the eerie feeling that she was being herded towards a place and time.

Pressing the gas pedal she started down the bumpy road. The trees towered over the truck like giants with arms raised as if to protect her from the falling night.

Finally she reached the end of the road, literally. There was nothing in front of her but branches and bark.

"Fine, just fuckin' fine!" Lura said.

She pounded her fists on the steering wheel in frustration, her anger evident in the honking of the horn.

Finally she bent her head to rest on the leather wrapped wheel in exhaustion.

"Dylan. Where are you baby?" she asked in a soft voice.

"Were you looking for my granddaughter?" asked a male voice from the left of her.

Startled, Lura looked up.

"What? Who?"

She glanced around in confusion finally looking out the window to see a copper colored face with black eyes staring back at her. She recognized that smile, and she recognized that face. Wiping her cheeks she snatched at the door handle.

"Gray Hawk!" she exclaimed. "Boy am I happy to see you." Lura stated as she open the door and slid out of the seat.

Gray Hawk was startled to find his arms full of a small giggling blond.

"I am very pleased to see you, Little Falcon, the

elderly man said, hugging the young woman. His heart soared with the knowledge that his granddaughter's mate had arrived and would now help her complete her quest.

Grabbing the suitcase from the back seat he wrapped his arm around the small shoulders and led the way.

"Come in little one, come in."

The cabin was filled with the smell of burning wood and the glow of a warm fire. Lura glanced around smiling at the obviously male décor. She could envision her Dylan growing up in this house, first a lanky teenager then a feisty defiant adolescent. She smiled as her mind pictured a younger version of her soul mate.

"Welcome to my home little one," said the old man.

He led Lura into the living room and to a seat by a dancing fire. Placing her luggage by the hall he walked slowly back into the living room pausing to turn on the heat under the ancient teakettle. He glanced into the room watching the young woman. She was a small and golden bird, alert and curious and he understood why his granddaughter was drawn to her. He watched as she paused in front of a picture of Dylan, her hand reached out to trace the image. He heard her whisper in a determined voice.

"I'm here Dylan. Don't worry baby, I'm here now."

The old warrior smiled, he saw the spirit of the falcon in this small blond. She would make a good mate for his granddaughter.

"Well, young one, I have put the kettle on and we

will have tea soon. While we wait I have a story to tell you, it is about a hawk and a falcon…"

CHAPTER 13

The dark sedan pulled into the parking lot of a small hotel; the driver stepped out and slammed the car door.

"Stupid piece of shit," he grumbled walking around the front of the car. He walked up the drive towards the hotel lobby, jerked the door open and strolled up to the desk. The attendant was on the phone giggling to someone on the other end. She looked up and noticed the tall blond man standing impatiently at the desk tapping his key on the counter top to attract her attention.

"Hold on a minute honey, some dick weed is demanding my presence," she sighed in irritation then placed the hand set on the desk and turned to the man.

"Yes? Do you want a room?" she asked staring at him coldly.

"What do you think? That I'm here for the fucking weather? I want a room for two nights. Is that gonna be too difficult for you to handle?" he stated, glaring at the young woman.

"Fine, that is $40.00 a night, pay in advance and if you want to use the phone that is extra," she said smiling at him.

He opened his wallet, pulled out four twenties and tossed them at the girl.

"Now give me a damn room."

The girl collected the cash and slipped it into her pocket. Turning, she reached for a key and tossed it to him.

"Room 124, go out the front and all the way to the end of the building. Ice machine is on the corner and check out is at eleven." She turned back to the phone and pick up the receiver.

"Now where were we? Oh yeah, well Karen told me last night…"

He frowned at the girl then turned and headed back out to his car.

"Stupid fuckin' bitch. This room better be nice for what I had to pay for it," he grumbled as he walked back to his car.

The young woman on the phone started to chuckle.

"Hey, Sue, that stupid dick weed just left. You remember that room we have the work order on? Yeah, the one with the leaky toilet and the air-conditioning that doesn't always work. Well, guess what room Prince Charming is staying in?"

Gray Hawk stood and walked slowly into the kitchen. Lura could hear the sound of plastic wrap, glasses rattling and the soft splashing of water. Moments later she could smell the scent of fresh brewed tea and hot bread.

The old man came back out with a small tray of toast and two large cups of tea.

"Can't tell a story without refreshments ya know," he said smiling.

He placed a steaming cup in front of Lura along with a paper towel with two thick slices of toast with melted butter.

Gray Hawk stared into the fire and began his story.

"The story has been handed down in our family for many generations. It has changed very little over the years. I remember when I told Dylan's mother the story and I am sure she told Dylan."

He poked the fire with an iron poker and collected his thoughts.

Lura sat quietly waiting for the elder to begin the story. She had heard that there was a tale of a Falcon and a Hawk and she was anxious to hear it but knew better that to push the old man.

"Well, let me see if I can remember it all" he began.

"Legends tell that many, many years ago when Mother Earth was new there existed two of every animal. They were told that they were to be the beginning of their kind on the planet. Each species found its mate and set about creating a home.

The powerful horse galloped off with a beautiful mare and soon returned with a small golden foal that looked just like him. The great eagle flew off with his mate and returned bragging that he had bested the horse and had two young ones. The graceful playful otter swam off with his mate and returned with three young and bragged to the others. The hawk flew through the sky with his mate and returned boasting of his four young. And so it went, each creature trying to outdo the other.

Now, of the creatures that lived on the earth, the raptors were the proudest of all. After all they commanded the winds and the sky. Of all the creatures surely they were the greatest. So for years each competed with the other. Year after year their young grew to adulthood and left their families finding mates and increasing their numbers.

Finally, they gathered to determine which bird was the greatest so it happened that the birds all met one day and decided to count their children, and grandchildren and great grand children. The great eagle screamed out a call and the sky was filled the beating of hundreds of wings. The great raptors blocked out the sun. Each was counted.

As the day went on each great bird of prey brought out their families. Finally it came down to the last two great raptors, the First Falcon and the First Hawk. Each called their children and counted, each one knew they had the largest number of children. All the other birds waited to see what would happen. As it turned out both had the same number of children and grand children and great grand children. So they decide that the only way to determine who was the greatest was to have a great battle. The Great Spirit had been watching all that was going on and became angry. He spoke out to the raptors.

"I have placed you here to live in peace. I will not

allow this battle to occur. Instead I will allow the youngest of each of your tribes to battle. The winner will prove that their tribe is the greatest."

Now, unknown to the Great Spirit, Mother Earth knew that the raptor's youngest children were one male and one female and she placed a love spell on the battlefield. The two battlers would be joined forever and one would not be able to survive without the other.

The Great Spirit, like Mother Earth, was very concerned. He knew that if no battle occurred then the great tribe of the raptors would set aside their competition and live in peace. He planned for the battle by blessing two young families. Days before the battle arrived two raptor families were blessed with hatchlings. There were four eggs in each nest and three had hatched from the hawk's nest and three from the falcon's nest. All had been large and powerful males; finally the last eggs began to crack. The hawk arrived first; a beautiful and powerful bird emerged from the egg. The First Hawk screamed out his pleasure, and the Great Spirit smiled for as he had planned, the young Hawk was a female. He believed that the female would not fight.

The falcon clan watched as each small falcon egg hatched. They flapped their long beautiful wings as each male emerged. Finally the last egg hatched and a beautiful little female emerged.

Now, each tribe waited for their young to grow until finally, the time arrived for the battle. Both tribes sent their youngest out to the battlefield. The great hawk had been trained to fight and knew that the pride of the hawk tribe rested on her powerful wings. She flew into the sky over the battleground, screaming out her challenge. In the distance she heard a high-pitched response. Into the sky came a beautiful swift winged falcon.

The hawk was stunned; she had never seen such a beautiful bird. She could not bring herself to battle the falcon.

The falcon saw the hawk and called out a challenge as she also had also been trained to battle.

With her talons outstretched she dove at the large hawk, determined to tear the other bird from the sky. She fell towards the hawk that had come to rest on a great stone, her breast exposed to the falcon.

The great hawk felt that if she were to die, it would be at the talons of this beautiful falcon.

As she got closer the falcon was struck by the beauty of the great hawk. She tried to stop her flight, but could not. In desperation she turned her wings at the last minute and struck the rock at the feet of the beautiful hawk and died.

Heartbroken at the death of the falcon the hawk threw herself from the rock tumbling through the sky and landing in the rocks next to the broken falcon.

Seeing the death of the two beautiful young birds, the raptor tribes realized how foolish they had been. They went to the Great Spirit to plead for their lives.

The Great Spirit was saddened; he had not planned for the death of the two beautiful birds.

'*I cannot bring back the two young raptors,*' he told the tribes, '*but into each generation two souls will be reborn. One will be soul of the Hawk and one will be the soul of the Falcon. And like your families they will mate for the duration of their time on Mother Earth. This I promise to the tribes of the raptors.*'

"So every generation we look for the spirit of the

Hawk and Falcon. We know that they will meet and nothing will come between the two mated souls."

Lura stared wide-eyed at Dylan's grandfather.

"Dylan calls me her Falcon. Does she think we are the reincarnated spirits of the two raptors?"

"No," the old man smiled. "She does not think you are the falcon, she knows it." He stated sipping his still warm tea.

The wolf nudged Dylan closer towards the doorway and out onto the open courtyard by the library. She watched as her father turned away from the parking lot and his car and walked out towards the park across from the library.

"Where the devil is he going?" she asked absentmindedly scratching the wolf's head.

She had not expected an answer and so was surprised when a voice responded in her head. *Why don't you follow him and find out, young pup. You might be surprised.*

"Humph, who are you calling a pup? I figure I am older than you even if you count your age in doggie years," she said smiling.

Don't bet on it pup, the voice responded.

I am much older than I look and I have followed you through several lifetimes. You humans are strange creatures. For some reason you seem to have to make life difficult.

The voice responded with a chuckle as the wolf nipped Dylan in the back of the leg.

"Hey! Watch it you. I thought you weren't suppose to feel pain in your sleep."

Well, that would be if you were having a regular dream. You, young one are on a vision quest. That is a bit different, the voice said.

Dylan walked forward following her father and rubbing her leg where she had been nipped. Looking down at the wolf that studiously ignored her and loped along at the woman's side, her tongue hanging out, the edge of her mouth turned up in a wolfish smile.

John Cameron walked through the park, his hands balled into fists and shoved into his pockets. He had done quite a bit of research and learned some things that he was not sure if he believed. He did however learn that it was important to the mental health of a young person to have the support of their family as they went through these changes. He finally realized that Dylan's preference for women was not something that she had a lot of control over. She had not set out to cause her family any pain or embarrassment, as he had initially thought.

It's just the way things are, he tried to reason with himself.

Finding a bench under a sheltering pine, he sat down and leaned forward clasping his hands together deep in concentration.

This could be a defining moment in his life. He had a serious choice to make and a lot of thinking to do before he made it. The last time he faced this type of crossroad he had opted for the easy, safe road and it had nearly cost him the woman he loved. Now here he was again back at that same fork in the road. His decisions could be complicated or they could be simple. It all depended on what he wanted...didn't it?

Dylan watched the younger version of her father.

He seemed to age before her eyes.

John sat thinking, not about this decision, but how to make the decision. What to base it on? Should he decide based on his career? The last time he did that he became a Senator and a very wealthy man, but that choice had cost him years with his wife and daughter.

Should he decide based on how the world would view the father of a lesbian? What would his peers think? His fellow Senators? Was it important? What about the people who had elected him into office? How would this affect his future? Was his future that critical? More so than his daughter?

Should he base this decision on his conscience? How did he really feel knowing that his daughter was gay?

All these thoughts raced through his mind. He bowed his head and felt his shoulders slump. Slowly it dawned on him, his daughter was missing! She had run away, because of him. First he abandoned her, then, when he finally did come home, he tried to force her to become someone she could never be. Now, based on what he had read, he was trying to control her very existence. *WRONG, WRONG, WRONG!* He sat up as if pulled upright on a puppeteers string. What had he been doing? These last few years had been the happiest and the most rewarding in his life because of his family. He realized now that he had pushed and pushed constantly trying to remake them. He was happy with his wife, she was loving and beautiful, his daughter was bright, attractive and popular. They had lived together happily before he had come back into their lives. Now he was ruining it all. Why? For the sake of his career and the feelings of a bunch of stuck up bureaucrats? He neglected his wife, no not neglected, ignored. He used her as a beautiful prop, part of his political arsenal, now he wanted to do the same thing to Dylan. He had chosen the easy path and had met with success, but at what cost? No, this time he would go the distance, he would support his family, no matter what, he would be there for his daughter.

What an insensitive jerk I have been. It has always been about me, what I want, what is best for me. I think it's time to think of my family. God, it took Dylan running away to make me really look at myself, John thought.

He had nearly lost his daughter because of his pigheaded, stubborn drive for fame. Then he realized, he **had** lost her, she was gone. He had finally learned an important lesson, but what had it cost him? His heart sank again. He looked up at the sky through the pine needles.

"Dylan? I am not sure where you are, but I am so sorry. If God lets me see you, again I swear, I will try to understand, I promise. God just give me the chance," he whispered.

A figure in the shadows wiped the tears from her eyes.

CHAPTER 14

Lura stared at Gray Hawk. "So if the legend is true, Dylan and I are soul mates," she said a smile in her voice.

The elder smiled, he had seen the dazed look of awe in the young woman's eyes.

"Gray Hawk," she stated, her voice sounding drawn and tired. "I love your granddaughter and I don't doubt that Dylan and I are suppose to be together. Since I have found her I can't imagine my life without her."

Lura looked into the empty cup of tea, surprised to realize she had finished it while listening to the story. She looked up into the black eyes of Gray Hawk.

"I know you and Dylan are very close. When she..." Lura's voice broke and she paused to collect herself. "When she left me, Dylan left a note. She said she would love me forever. I believe her, but if she does not want me, if she wants to be left alone, she needs to tell me, face to face."

Lura stopped here, her throat tightening. She looked again at the empty cup wishing that more tea would mysteriously appear to ease her throat.

"I know that Dylan would have come here, come

home to you. Please can you tell me where she is? I know she needs me," Lura pleaded.

Gray Hawk stood and walked to the fire where he stared into the flames.

"Lura Grant, do you have any idea what my granddaughter has been through? She came here to soothe her soul. Her body has been broken and her mind is confused. She sees the enemy around her and fears for her own sanity. Her nights are tormented with the dreams of those she has killed. She sees their deaths over and over again. Now she has a chance to regain control to and heal her mind. What makes you think that your presence will not cause her more harm and undo the healing that has already begun? If she left you, maybe that is what she wants. Why should I go against her wishes?" He turned to face Lura, an angry scowl on his face.

Lura was confused, why was he keeping her away from Dylan? She had not come all this way to be stopped here so close to the woman she loved. Dylan was in trouble, she could feel it and no one, not her mother and not even Dylan's Grandfather, was going to keep them apart. If Dylan didn't want her fine, but she had damn well better tell her that herself.

Gray Hawk watched as the frightened, confused and desperate expression left Lura's face.

She stood slowly from the chair, placed the cup on the table and walked towards the fireplace. She leaned forward, her hands resting close together on the mantle, her forehead resting on the backs of her hands. She stared into the fire, drawing the heat into her lungs, fueling her anger.

Gray Hawk saw her shoulders slump then watched

as the small woman took in a deep breath and began to speak. Each word fell on his ears hard and distinct. She turned, her head still down, her fists balled as she walked towards him. Her voice was cold, soft, with a much more pronounced Southern accent.

"The way I see it Gray Hawk, this is not your decision to make, it is mine, mine and Dylan's. I was there when she was going through some of that killin'. I was there for her when she was wounded and while she struggled everyday, to regain enough strength just to stand. She saved my life and the way I see it I owe her the chance to heal. But I know Dylan, she is as stubborn as she is brave and she needs me now whether she knows it or not."

Lura stopped here and looked up into Gray Hawk's challenging eyes. "

"I love Dylan and she owns my heart, I will be damned if I am gonna leave her now."

Gray Hawk was amazed at the strength in the small woman.

"Let me make sure you understand this right now, I am not going to let you or anyone else drive me off."

She stepped closer to the old man.

"Yep, the way I see it you got two options. You either tell me where I can find her or I will call out every damn Forest Ranger this side of the Carolinas and we will start scouring these woods for her. And believe me Gray Hawk, I will personally pull up every DAMN tree and look behind every DAMN blade of grass until I find her! Dylan needs me and by God I am gonna be there for her. You can either help me or get the HELL OUT OF MY WAY!"

Lura was now as close to nose to nose as her five foot four inch frame would allow. Her eyes were hard dark chips of emerald. Her brow was furrowed with anger and determination.

Gray Hawk did not back down.

"Well, how do you plan on doing that?" he asked, pressing in closer to the angry blond.

"There are no phones in this cabin and I have been told that this is what is called a dead zone for those small mobile phones. So how do you plan on calling your Rangers?"

Lura stared back at the old man.

"With fuckin' smoke signals if I have to!" She said her eyes still flashing angrily.

She was totally unprepared for the response; Gray Hawk threw back his head and laughed.

Her brow furrowed and her eyes closed in tight slits as she placed her hands on her hips and stared up angrily at him.

He continued to laugh, tears streaking his face. He sat down on his chair holding his sides, bursting into fresh bouts of laughter whenever he looked up at her.

"What, may I ask, is so funny?" she asked, very obviously peeved.

"I am sorry Lura Grant, but I can picture you, standing over an open fire, great puffs of smoke billowing out," the old man said, wiping the tears from his eyes.

"I see now why my granddaughter calls you Little Falcon. You are as fierce and protective as that small sky warrior. You are a good match for my Dylan; maybe you can tame that woman down."

Lura smiled at the old man. She had no intention

of taming Dylan; she liked her just the way she was so she simply grinned at Gray Hawk and kept her opinion to herself.

Still chuckling, the old man walked out of the room and returned several minutes later. In his hands he held a hand drawn map. Waving at Lura to join him he spread the map on the table and began tracing a path.

"We are here." He said pointing to a small star shaped marking on the map.

"If you go in this direction you will find a deer path, somewhere near here. Follow it to a clearing, Dylan is there."

"Why is she in the forest, Grandfather? Is she so determined to escape from the rest of the world?" Lura was concerned. If Dylan wanted her to stay away, if she didn't want the world to find her, then maybe it was best she wait here. Dylan would come out when she was ready.

Gray Hawk though about what Lura was asking.

"Little Falcon, it is not Dylan who makes this decision, it is the Great Spirit. It guides Dylan's life, it calls you to her and you must follow, it is your destiny to be at Dylan's side."

Lura stared at the old man, then down at the sketch.

He has got to be kidding, she thought.

Her eyes traveled from the paper to the old warriors' smiling face.

Guess not. She grinned back.

"You had better rest tonight and start out at first light. The path is not visible in the dark and if you miss it you could be lost in that forest for a very long time," Gray Hawk said rolling the map and handing it to Lura.

Lura took the map holding it close to her chest and smiled at Gray Hawk. "Thank you Grandfather. I will bring Dylan home safe, believe me."

In the small, humid hotel room Nathan kicked the rattling air conditioner in disgust.

"Damn piece of shit! I know that bitch at the desk knew this thing didn't work."

He walked over to the battered nightstand and picked up the room phone ready to dial the front desk.

"Damn, damn, damn!" He slammed the dead phone down sat on the bed and reached for his shoes.

"Wait 'til I see her. Who does she think she is dealing with? I won't stand for this. First no air and now no damn phone!"

He stood and walked out of the room, forgetting that motel doors lock automatically when shut. He jerked around quickly and made a grab for the handle, just missing.

"Fuck!" he screamed then turned back towards the front of the motel. Now thoroughly angry he stomped towards the front door. Reaching the outer door he snatched at the handle and discovered the outer door was locked. He looked through the glass and saw the attendant still on the phone her back to him. He banged on the door, and watched as the girl, her back still to him, wave her hand at the No Vacancy sign. Apparently the door was sound proof.

"ARRRGGGHHH!!!!" Nathan turned and sat on the ground outside the door and waited for the girl to get off the phone.

CHAPTER 15

Lura stood silently in the forest, surrounded by wooden giants. It was truly a beautiful place. Sipping from her bottle of water she smiled thinking of her lover close by and in such a peaceful setting. The trees were beautiful, a mixture of evergreen, oak and, unless her nose deceived her, a cedar or two.

She glanced down at the hand drawn map to recheck her location. Based on the drawings there was supposed to be a trail near her that lead to a clearing and Dylan.

Putting her water back in her pack, Lura stared down at the map again. She hefted the pack onto her back and leaning the wooden walking stick against her shoulder glanced up to get her bearings.

For some reason Grandfather had decided that she needed a bit of assistance in making it through the forest. The long wooden stick he had given her was fairly lightweight and had actually come in handy. She had poked the bushes before she passed making sure that no slimy, creepy, hairless and legless things were in her path. She shuddered at the thought of snakes.

Not far behind Nathan followed, but his path was not as easily traversed, seemed the trees continued to jump in front of him, but he was determined to keep Lura in sight. "Damn her she did have to go into the woods. Thank you Lura Grant!" he exclaimed to no one in particular.

Why couldn't she run away to Tahiti or Barcelona? The woods. The damn, stinkin' woods. What the hell could she be looking for in the woods? Well, it sure wasn't that old man; I know she didn't sleep with him. What the hell would he have to offer a girl like her? She needs a real man, like me not some old shriveled up old goat. Humm, maybe that's why she's here. Maybe she found some young Forest Ranger or young buck. Well, I can take care of him, whoever he is. I was the Winchester Club Boxing champ two years in a row.

Nathan puffed out his chest a bit very sure of his physical prowess. He stepped over a fallen tree and paused. He had finally caught up with Lura and watched as she stared at a large piece of paper. Apparently there was someplace in particular she was heading and she had a map. He waited as she checked the terrain and compared it to the map then picked up her walking stick and disappeared into the forest.

"What the...where did she go?"

Nathan stepped out onto the trail and stared at the trees that appeared to be a solid wall of wood. How could she have just disappeared? She had just been standing here. He looked down but was not able to see anything in the fallen leaves.

"Damn, damn, damn!" he swore running his

manicure fingers through his tousled hair in frustration. He had never excelled in these sorts of outdoor activities.

He paced back and forth for several minutes before deciding to head in the general direction he had last seen Lura.

Forcing branches aside he stepped into the tree line.

Lura followed the deer trail deeper into the woods. Each step, she knew was bringing her closer and closer to Dylan.

The forest was incredible, the morning was fresh and even though it was late August, it was comfortably cool. She strolled along her mind on her missing soul mate as she stepped into a large clearing. She stopped, breathless at the sight. A single large cedar seemed to dominate the clearing next to it was a small wood covered shelter, smoke curling from an opening in its top and a trail of stones led to a covered doorway. To the right of the shelter was a neat camp, the set up all to familiar to the blond.

She stepped into the clearing and towards the camp area, dropping her bag next to the circle of stones that marked the center of the camp.

"Well, Dylan must be in that little hut, the question is should I wait here or go on in? Humph, like that is really a question. I haven't seen my woman in weeks and she is just on the other side of that doorway."

Lura stooped down and crawled into the hut pausing for a second to allow her eyes to adjust to the darkness. It was more the site before her than the steam in the small hut that took her breath away.

Stretched out on a pallet of cedar branches and fall leaves lay Dylan, naked. Her skin, covered in a soft sheen of sweat and resembled molten bronze in the dim light. Her black hair soaked and curled around her shoulders and cheeks, her chest rising and falling with each steady breath.

Lura was stunned; she had almost forgotten how beautiful Dylan was. Slowly she crawled forward, careful not to waken the sleeping woman as she gazed down at the still face. When was the last time she had seen Dylan like this? Their hotel room in Georgia, the night before Dylan had left her, but even then she had not had this calm still look on her face. She had been tormented and confused. She had been so tense that she feared her own actions.

Now here she was close enough to touch.

Lura watched as Dylan's eyes fluttered as if on the edge of a deep dream. She wanted desperately to wake her, but she remembered reading somewhere that it was not safe to wake someone from a trance or deep sleep. So she sat back and waited, content to be so close to her soul mate.

Nathan winced as yet another branch reached out and slapped him in the face. "These woods must be cursed. Why else would I be going through all this just to find one small blonde?"

He swore as he wiped his face and struggled through the thick brush. Finally he reached a clearing and he was about to step through when a movement caught his eye. He watched as Lura stepped into the clearing near him. Amazed at her pristine appearance, he was tempted to confront her, when he saw her face light up at the discovery of the small shelter in the clearing. Lura dropped her pack and walked to the shelter.

He watched as she mumbled something to herself and seemed to pause for a minute to make up her mind. Then to his utter amazement she knelt on the ground and crawled into the shelter. He waited for some sound to come from the small wood and mud hut, but nothing happened.

"Whoever built that thing must not be around. Well, that suits me just fine. I'll just sit here and wait until he comes back. If he thinks he is going to steal my woman, he has another thought coming."

Nathan looked around for a likely spot to settle in and finding a moss-covered boulder, he crawled on top and made himself comfortable.

Lura smiled as she watched Dylan sleep. She was glad beyond reason that she had finally found her. She was concerned about the depth of the sleep though. It was obvious that the dreams the soldier was having were disturbing, she moaned in her sleep and, at times tears rolled from her eyes.

Lura reached out to touch her more than once, but the thought of the hot coffee incident back at the hotel stopped her from waking the sleeping woman. As time wore on she found herself becoming drowsy.

Must be the heat in here, she thought. *I'll just stretch out for a while and take a quick nap. That way I will be here when Dylan wakes up.*

Lura took off her shoes and carefully stepped over the steaming rocks and lay next to Dylan. Minutes later she was sound asleep. Her body, sensing the presence of the woman she loved, slipped closer and wrapped an arm around a naked waist.

Lura wiggled closer in her sleep and rested her head on Dylan's shoulder. With a sigh, both women drifted deeper into sleep.

Dylan watched her father walk away. She wanted to reach out and touch him. He really had wanted to make things right.

She felt a nudge on her hand and glanced down at the wolf, her blue gray eyes stared back at her.

Yes, he regrets his actions young cub, but he needed time to realize his loss before he could accept such change.

Again she heard the voice in her head, but this time it was comforting.

"I see that now, Wolf. I will try to forgive him. It is over and time to settle old wounds," she said.

He is a stubborn man with a very strong will much like his totem, the badger. But like the badger he is very determined and will not leave a trail until his quarry is caught.

The voice continued. *"A bit like your mate."*

"My mate?" she asked

She looked again in the direction her father had taken but the scene had changed again.

A heavy fog had covered the area, golden and warm. She heard a sound in the distance. It was the beating of wings, then a piercing cry. She looked up to see a large hawk circling above. The hawk's cry was chilling and almost poignant. She watched as it drifted lazily in the golden fog, its powerful wings holding it aloft on some unseen, unfelt thermal. She did not see its wings move but still she heard the beating of wings.

The hawk called again, this time the sound was answered by a higher longer call.

Dylan squinted to see through the haze. It started as a small speck but rapidly grew. It was another raptor, a beautiful swift winged falcon. The hawk spotted the smaller bird and cried out again. Folding its wings the falcon dove down towards the large hawk.

Dylan was sure they would fight, but at the last second the hawk rolled over, talons extended and gripped the talons of the falcon. The two birds tumbled through the air, their wings held out their cries intertwined. As they grew closer to her they finally separated and climbed together. She watched as they flew higher and higher until they were out of sight.

She started to turn towards the wolf again to ask him the reason for the aerial display when she felt a presence drawing her. She felt hot, her head throbbed and her throat was dry. She struggled now against the golden fog, fighting the clinging mist.

Lura awoke to the moans and struggles of the woman in her arms.

"Dylan? Honey, wake up. Dylan?" Lura sat up, awakened by the thrashing and heat coming from the woman next to her. Alarmed now, Lura rolled to her knees. She reached for the struggling woman.

"Dylan, please, wake up."

She placed her hand on the hot forehead. Dylan was burning up. She moaned and thrashed about struggling against some dream that held her tight.

Lura stroked the damp forehead. She had been right; Dylan did indeed need her. She crawled from the sweat hut and, still barefooted, trotted to her pack. Snatching it up she slowed only long enough to grab

Dylan's canteen on her way back into the hut.

Nathan watched, growing drowsy waiting for something, anything, to happen. Lura had been inside the small hut for what seemed like hours and he looked up surprised when he heard a disturbance. Lura came scrambling out of the hut, rushed to her pack and grabbed it and her canteen. Without a backwards glance she rushed back into the hut.

"That bitch, she's been in there with him all this time!" He was angry, Lura had always portrayed the image of the innocent when she was whoring around all that time. Well he would take care of her once they were married, but for now he needed to take care of this rival.

Nathan stood and brushed off his trousers. He prepared to face the man inside the hut. He stepped forward out of the tree line but paused.

What the hell am I doing? I have no idea what this guy looks like or how big he is. He may have a weapon. Yes, I had better wait until I know what I am facing. Yeah, that would be a better plan.

He assured himself that his actions were more prudent than cowardly. He made a hasty departure making sure not to disturb the two in the small hut but also making sure he left a trail to follow back, and he planned on coming back. Lura Grant was too important to him, or rather her money was.

Inside the shelter Lura opened her pack pulling out a small bottle of aspirin, her water bottle, a towel and a washcloth. She lifted the now prone body and placed the pack under Dylan's head and shoulders.

Lura popped open the aspirin and shook two out into her palm.

There is no way in hell she is gonna be able to swallow these, Lura thought, staring at the small white tablets.

She opened her pack and pulled out her water bottle. She poured most of the contents onto the towel and washcloth and then she dropped in the two tablets. While they dissolved she wrapped the towel around Dylan's body and gently wiped her face with the washcloth.

The heat inside the small hut was almost unbearable. Lura looked up and saw that the majority of the smoke was leaving in a thin stream through the top of the hut, but the heat stayed inside.

She crawled to the door of the shelter and propped it open allowing some of the heat to escape and bringing the temperature inside to an almost bearable level.

"Dylan, open your mouth, Honey," she coaxed gently.

As the lips parted Lura dripped some of the melted aspirin and water into Dylan's mouth, rubbing her throat to encourage her to swallow.

"Good girl. Now rest, I'm not going anywhere."

She laid the towel over Dylan's overheated body and poured the remaining contents of the canteen over it, trying desperately to bring her body temperature down. She would need more water and quickly.

She crawled back out of the hut again and stood listening, the map she had gotten from Gray Hawk had shown a small pool of water near the area he had marked as the clearing she now stood in.

Lura closed her eyes, trying to focus all her attention on her hearing. There, I hear it!"

She turned and headed to her right. Forcing her way through the brush she stumbled into a small deep stream of fresh water that led to a pool. It was cold, washed down from the mountain's melting snow and mixing with a fresh water spring.

Lura filled the canteen and paused long enough to splash cold water onto her face. A quick flash of silver caught her eye. *Fish, fresh food for Dylan, and all I have to do is...*

She leaned forward and reached out, her eyes following the sleek swift fish. "I just have to grab one and it's fish fry for me and my baby." Lura concentrated on the movement as she brought her hand closer to the water. That is when she noticed the small fish had begun to congregate under her shadow. As she watched the school of tiny fish gather she noticed a large fish darted towards her drawn to the school of minnows and the prospect of an easy meal.

She waited, slowly lowering her hand closer and closer to the water, one quick movement and she had it. She drew her hand out throwing the fish onto the grass.

"Ha! Yeah, fish tonight!"

Lura jumped to her feet and did a little jig, staring down at the flopping fish.

With the canteen in one hand and the fish in the other she headed back towards camp.

Carefully Lura prepared the fish gutting it and placing it over the fire to cook. She went back into the shelter to check on Dylan and was pleased to discover that her temperature was falling. She poured more water on the washcloth and wipe her lovers face. Dylan's lips curved into a smile as the cool cloth touched her face.

Lura anxiously watched for any other indication that her lover would wake. She could be patient; they had a lifetime ahead of them.

Nathan sat in his hotel room, hot dirty and tired, the noise of the constantly dripping toilet had kept him awake all night.

He had finally gotten back to his hotel room after a day of hell in the forest and the air conditioning still wasn't working.

"That stupid heifer at the desk hasn't called in the repair for this damn thing yet. And I know I told her about the toilet. Just wait; when I get the money I will buy this stinking hole just so I can make her clean this room. Just before I fire her."

He smiled thinking of the young receptionist sweating in the heat of the room then begging him for her job.

"Wait, what if she decides to marry that other guy," he spoke aloud to himself.

"If Lura decides on him then he'll get my money! No, that is not gonna happen. I gotta stop him," Nathan said. "I gotta figure out what to do about him."

That night Lura sat up with Dylan, waiting for her to open her eyes. She had been to the pool several times refilling the canteen and her water bottle. She kept rewetting the towel, dissolving tablets and keeping her face wiped.

What seemed like days, but was only hours, passed and finally Dylan's eyes fluttered. Slowly, painfully Dylan struggled through the golden haze. The falcon called her soul and she had no choice but to respond.

Lura held her breath as she watched the blue eyes she loved focus on hers.

"Lura?" The voice was harsh and so softly spoken she was forced to lean closer to hear. She felt a hand slip into her hair and her lips were captured by her soul mate's.

Dylan could not resist the tempting site above her. She reached up, pulling the beautiful angel to her. As their lips touched she felt her heart soar. She opened her eyes and knew that things were right, her falcon had found her and she was home.

CHAPTER 16

Gray Hawk pressed the button disconnecting the mobile phone.

Wonderful things these mobile phone, but really bad reception. Maybe we really are in a dead zone. He chuckled thinking of the tale he had told Little Falcon. She was indeed a fierce little warrior.

He placed the phone back on Dylan's bed, the conversation he had just had was enlightening. Lura had come here even after her mother cancelled her flight. Harrison Grant had a great deal to say about that. Gray Hawk laughed aloud remembering the triad of creative terms Harrison had come up with to describe his feeling on that particular topic. Yes, he knew where Little Falcon got her temper.

Gray Hawk walked back out through the living room, picked up his staff and headed for the front door. It was time for his morning hike. Stepping out onto the front porch he closed his eyes and inhaled deeply smiling as he enjoyed the smell of the fresh air in his lungs. He paused; his eyes still closed and tilted his head. Something odd was going on.

Listening carefully, the old man tried to

understand what his ears and now his nose were telling him.

A storm was coming, but this was not a regular storm. He listened again trying to pick up familiar sounds. There were none. No birds, no insects and no wind in the leaves. Everything was still...too still. This was not a good sign. He bent to examine the little worker ants at his feet. As he watched they stopped their usual activities of food gathering, and had begun piling large grains of sand and clay at the entrance of their home. They were shutting the door, preparing for a storm. As he watched he saw the ants carry large bits of clay deep into the hole this was followed by sand and dirt. They were not just shutting the door; they were stopping up the entrance ensuring that nothing got past the plug. This was not just a storm; this was something much worse.

Nathan lay on his bed thinking of how he could prevent his rival from stealing his fortune. He had thought of challenging the man, but he had no idea how big this fellow was. He could get his ass whipped if the guy was big enough. No, maybe he needed to see what this guy looked like, maybe learn a bit about him and then he could plan.

He rose from the bed and grabbed his bag, tossing it onto the adjacent bed. The much-abused Samsonite still retained its good looks and strong locks.

Nathan slipped his key in and turned, though the locks were very good they were also very stiff. After banging repeatedly on the small silver clasp the lock finally gave and he opened the bag. Inside were several items of clothing, all of very good quality and in fine condition.

"One must keep up appearances," he mumbled to himself.

This time he was going prepared. He pulled out a pair of 501's, a pair of tan jock socks, a beige polo shirt and a light tan canvas LL Bean vest. He reached into the bag again and retrieved a brown belted shoulder holster and reaching under the piles of clothes to retrieve his Ruger 9mm. Checking the magazine, he slipped it into the butt of the pistol, pulled back the slide and chambered a round. Smiling, he re-holstered the pistol and laid it next to the clothes. Then he picked up a towel and headed for the shower.

Lura sat inside the small sweat hut feeding bits of fish to a still naked Dylan. She was a very happy camper and unable to remove the smile from her face.

Dylan had tried to get dressed but her clothing had disappeared, and strangely enough, she wasn't complaining.

Dylan leaned back relaxing as Lura carefully picked bits of fresh cooked fish from the bones and hand fed them to her. She had been here now for almost four days and this was the first bit of food she had eaten since the vision quest had started. She was not sure how Lura had found her but she was too happy to care. Right now the only thing that concerned her was eating, Lura had promised to help her with her bath once she finished her dinner, so hell or high water she was gonna eat every last bit of that damn fish.

Lura had it all planned; she would heat up some water in one of Dylan's tin cups then give her lover a relaxing sponge bath. Her lover was weak but gaining strength with every bite and she was determined to have Dylan back on her feet as soon as possible.

Or maybe I will get her back on her back as soon as possible. Oh Lura, you are soooo bad, the blonde thought with a grin.

Dylan watched her mate meticulously pick and de-bone pieces of fish careful to remove all of the tiny translucent bones. Why this would make Lura grin so foolishly she was not sure but *whatever makes her happy.*

That evening a freshly washed Dylan lay in front of a warm fire wrapped in a blanket as Lura gently combed her hair. The feel of the comb sliding through the long stands followed by Lura's gentle fingers was very soothing, very soothing.

Lura had enjoyed bathing her lover and was looking forward to a pleasant evening. She sat behind Dylan carefully untangling her long hair and enjoying the warmth of the fire, her mind on the events she hoped would occur later that evening. She was so preoccupied that she was taken completely off guard when she heard the soft sound of Dylan's snores.

"No," she whispered. "Not now, not tonight." She leaned forward and glanced down into the sleeping face of the exhausted woman.

Well, so much for the romantic plans. Lura thought with a sigh.

Standing she gently rolled Dylan over onto her side, the movement did not even wake her. Lura stared at the sleeping woman and realized how much she had missed the sound of Dylan's gentle snore. Smiling to herself she quickly removed her outer clothing and grabbing her blanket she lay down, covering them both and wrapping her arms around Dylan, she was soon

174

asleep.

Neither woman had noticed the darkening of the sky and both were asleep when the first gentle breezes began.

Gray Hawk was surprised to hear the sound of a car door slamming, he knew of no one who would be out near him at this time of day, especially with the storm coming. He knew it was not Dylan; she had enough sense to find shelter for herself and Lura.

The old warrior glanced out the front window still a bit surprised to have a visitor. "Who the devil would be out in the weather this time of day? Probably some tourist that has lost their way or something," the old man mused aloud.

He opened the door only to be greeted by the barrel of a pistol brandished by a young white man. Alarmed, he backed up, allowing the young man to push the door open and walk in. He wasn't sure what the fellow wanted; he had nothing in the house of any significant value.

He started to mention that to the young man when he felt the first blow. Falling to the floor, Gray Hawk looked up stunned and surprised. That was when he first noticed the look in the man's eyes.

Nathan was tired of the chase, he wanted what was rightfully his and Lord help anyone that stood in his way. Now he needed information and this old man was going to give it to him.

"Get up, you old man, I have some questions and you are going to answer them," he snarled. He motioned towards the living room with the pistol indicating to Gray Hawk to precede him. They sat on the chairs, which, earlier that week, had been occupied by Gray Hawk and Lura. Sitting by the fire Nathan turned and smiled at the blood he spotted trickling through the gray hair.

"Okay you old goat, I need to know who my woman is seeing in the woods. Is that your son out there she's shacked up with or some other young buck?"

Silence filled the air.

Nathan was not in the mood to play, he wanted answers now. He pulled back the slide and was startled to see a round fly by, he had forgotten he had chambered a round already. Grinning he looked up at the old man.

"Well, now you know there are real bullets in here old man.

Leaning forward he stared into the black eyes that even at his age, appeared clear and alert.

Now, I am not a real patient fellow, so if you don't mind, I am waiting. Who is Lura with in the woods? What's he like?"

Gray Hawk frowned, his heartbeat picked up at the mention of Lura's name. *This boy wants Lura and he is asking about Dylan. I don't know if Dylan is in any shape to handle him. She is on quest and is probably very weak now. Maybe I can stall.*

"What makes you think I know who Lura is?" Gray Hawk questioned, staring at the frustrated would-be suitor.

Nathan looked at the old man and smiled, he calmly pointed the pistol at Gray Hawk and pulled the trigger. The report was booming in the small room.

Gray Hawk felt the round tear through his arm as he fell backwards onto the floor by the force of the impact.

"I told you old man, I really am not patient. Now, I am going to ask you again, and I will shoot you in the other arm if you don't tell me." Nathan grinned, he was really enjoying this, why hadn't he thought of this earlier? He pointed the pistol at the old man again, tapping his foot impatiently.

Gray Hawk looked up from the floor. *This man is insane.* If he told him about Dylan this man would try to kill her. He had to stop him.

"Don't, old man. I can see it in your eyes. Believe me I will kill you and then I will kill the man with Lura. Just tell me so you can live." Nathan sneered; he was getting tired of waiting. He aimed at the old man again a pulled the trigger. This time the bullet ripped through his leg.

"Surprise," Nathan laughed

The pain was incredible. Gray Hawk fell back clutching his leg with a scream of agony, his body twitching in response to the pain. He heard ringing in his ears and then nothing.

Nathan stared down at the unconscious man in disgust. "Some warrior you turned out to be old man, you couldn't even take a bullet or two." He holstered his weapon, turned and without a look back strolled out the front door, blissfully unaware of the dark gray clouds rolling overhead. A storm was brewing.

Dylan woke in a cold sweat; something was wrong. She sat up and stared around at the strange surroundings, initially disoriented. She felt a heaviness on her body and, glancing down, saw Lura laying beside her. The blond had one arm hanging onto her blanket and the other draped possessively over Dylan's waist. The picture filled her heart but she was certain that the smaller woman's presence had not cause the reaction, that pulled her from her deep sleep.

Dylan glanced around; the forest was trying to tell her something. Looking up she watched as greenish black clouds began rolling across the sky. The giant pine trees bent, swaying in the heavy wind. Tilting her head she sniffed the air, a heavy rain was coming she could smell it. But it wasn't just the rain; there were no animal noises. No birds, no frogs, no bugs, nothing. The forest was virtually still except for the trees that swayed back and forth and the sound of the wind.

"Oh shit!" Dylan exclaimed.

Now she knew what was happening, this was not just was a big storm on its way and the animals had already taken refuge to ride it out. They knew that this was a different kind of storm. She had to find some shelter for Lura fast; the way the wind was picking up it was going to be a bad one.

She reached down and shook the small shoulder next to her.

"Lura, Lura honey wake up," she called gently. She really loved having the other woman with her, even in this kind of weather.

"No! Dylan, don't leave me. Please don't leave me," Lura mumbled in her sleep.

Dylan listened to the girl's pleas frowning, realizing how much she had hurt Lura. At the time she hadn't even thought about Lura's feelings when she abandoned the other woman. She had simply left a note and disappeared.

Her only thoughts were to get away. She had lied to herself and to Lura. Telling the woman she loved that she was afraid that she might hurt her wasn't a complete lie, but she knew that deep inside she would rather die than hurt Lura. The truth was that her only concern when she left was for her own pain. Her guilt for living when her men were all dead, the pain of living to kill, it had all come back to torment her and she had not been able to bear it. She had run.

Now she knew that leaving Lura was the wrong thing to do, Lura would have helped her bear the burden and eventually would have helped her overcome the nightmares. If only she had told her the truth. Well, they had a lot to talk about when they were out of this mess. She smiled at the idea that if possible, she intended to spend the rest of her life telling her how much she loved her. The short time they had already had was not enough.

No it wasn't, a voice spoke in her mind.

That voice, it's familiar, Dylan thought, looking around.

There at the edge of the forest was a large figure, as she watched a wolf stepped out into the open. It stared at her with blue white eyes, its tongue lolling out in a wolfish grin. Dylan stared back gape jawed. She started to rise and go to the wolf when another sound drew her attention.

Glancing to her left she saw a strange man step out of the woods. He stared at her frowning, then down at Lura. *His eyes* Dylan though, *they aren't right.*

The stranger reached inside his jacket and drew out a pistol. Dylan's eyes grew large as she stared at the big bore gun. Slowly she stood hoping that her naked frame would draw his eyes from Lura.

"Who are you? What do you want?" she asked, stepping between the stranger and the sleeping woman, her eyes focused on his.

"Humm, funny you should ask," Nathan said walking carefully out into the open, his eyes taking in the full breasts and the long naked legs.

"I came here for her," he said, waving the gun in Lura's direction his eyes never leaving the naked body in front of him. He had been a bit surprised when the tall beauty moved to position herself between him and the still sleeping blond.

"Well, well, what have we here? You afraid I'm going to shoot...your girlfriend?" he sneered, pointing the gun down between Dylan's legs that were now straddling the sleeping woman.

"I would have never taken her for queer, but she did turn me down back at the mall." Nathan said musing aloud and rubbing his cheek as if still feeling the sting of the slap.

Dylan's eyes grew cold as she listened to the man.

"No wonder that old man back at the cabin wouldn't tell me who she was seeing," he laughed, his voice carried away in the growing force of the wind.

"Hope he wasn't important to ya." He grinned when he noticed the angry look he was receiving from the dark woman. "Hope he wasn't some sort of Chief or something. He didn't die well. Really begged me not to shoot him," Nathan lied, seeing that his words were having an effect on the dark haired woman.

"Pain?" he taunted, "Do I see pain in your eyes? You are trying to steal what belongs to me," Nathan said gesturing at Lura.

"That is my property and you need to step away,

now." He said, pointing the pistol at the dark woman.

Dylan could not believe what she had heard. Gray Hawk was dead? *No, my grandfather is a warrior and this man lies.*

"Liar!" Dylan yelled over the sound of the rising wind, stepping forward with each word.

"My grandfather is Chief Gray Hawk, War Chief of the Cherokee Nation. A Hawk would never beg. You are a liar. And Lura belongs to no man. She is my mate and you will not touch her," Dylan screamed.

She had been able to move closer to the strange man but stopped when he redirected the pistol at her. Her eyes narrowed as she stared at him, her head pounding with the pictures his words had drawn in her mind. She felt heat radiating from her body even in the now chilled wind. Her focus narrowed, blocking out everything but the man in front of her. He became the embodiment of all her torment and pain. He may have harmed her grandfather and had tried to claim Lura. That would not happen.

Nathan watched the woman's eyes; they changed from light blue to almost black as her pupils grew large. Her brow furrowed and her hair, picked up by the wind, seemed alive and writhing around her shoulders and waist. Slowly a grim smile appeared on her lips and she began to walk towards him. He pointed the gun at her.

"Stop right there or I swear, I will shoot you," he yelled, confident in the power of the threat.

He was stunned when she ignored him and continued forward.

Dylan could hear nothing but the wind. It sounded different, more like the howl of a wolf. She prowled forward slowly anxious to have this threat terminated.

Nathan backed up, his mind telling him that this woman was different and that she was not afraid of him.

"What is wrong with you? I told you, I will shoot you." Now his eyes widened with fear as the strange woman threw back her head and laughed. When she returned her gaze at him he was chilled by her eyes, they had changed again; her pupils had shrunk to a pinpoint. Focusing her eyes on his throat, eyes that had now gone from a dark storm blue to silver, her face still wreathed in a feral grin.

Fear gripped Nathan. He felt his stomach roll and the taste of bile was in his throat. He had never dreamed of facing anything like this. His heart raced, as his mind tried to find a way to win out. He had to keep this woman away from him.

He pulled the trigger, but she kept coming. He fired again...nothing. He knew the gun had fired, he felt the recoil as it kicked in his hand.

Dylan saw the flash of the pistol and felt the bullets as they whistled past her ear. Nathan's fear was making him shake, throwing off his aim. Dylan knew that if she shook him up enough he would become so rattled that his aim would be fucked, but that would correct itself as she got closer.

Can't be helped, she thought.

Suddenly, something flew past her and straight at Nathan. It knocked him to the ground and sent the gun flying.

The sounds of the gunfire had awakened Lura. Rolling over, she watch in shock as Nathan fired at her soulmate. What was he doing here? Who in the hell did he think he was, firing at her Dylan?

She watched first stunned then relieved as Nathan missed again. Her relief was soon replaced with anger when Nathan leveled the pistol to fire again. She knew Dylan, her Hawk, would not stop until one of them was down.

Leaping to her feet she charged past Dylan and threw herself at Nathan. Her teeth rattled as she slammed into the heavier body. She felt them both fall as she impacted with him. She tried to roll so that she would be on top, but he forced her over with is greater strength. He leaned over her, one arm drawn back and she prepared herself for the blow, hoping to be able to fight him long enough for Dylan to get the gun.

The weight of his body on hers was cutting off her wind and he struck out at her, a blow landing with stunning force on her jaw. She saw lights flashing behind her eyes as the pressure of his weight was suddenly pulled off of her.

Dylan had reached the fallen couple seconds after Lura's flying tackle. Her anger had fed her body with adrenaline as she reached down and picked Nathan up by his hair. Drawing her fist back she buried it in his face, smiling at the satisfying crunching sound of breaking teeth. Even as she felt the skin on her knuckles tear, she pulled back again and swung up, catching him in the chest directly under his rib cage causing his legs to buckle.

Nathan fell to the ground with his head spinning from the force of the blow that knocked the air from his lungs.

Coming to his knees, he reached up and, cupping his hand, spit three teeth into his palm.

"You BITCH!" he yelled in an angry lisp. He charged forward, his shoulder down his arm grabbing the naked waist he took Dylan to the ground.

Lura stood in the high winds watching her lover fight the larger Nathan. She silently cheered when she saw him go down, but was frightened when he rose and tackled Dylan.

Lura started forward intent on joining her lover in the fight when she realized that the force of the wind had picked up. She stared up stunned to see the tops of the trees bending and twisting. Their branches seemed to glow as they were outlined against a blue-black sky. The sound around her was more of a roar than the usual bluster of a storm. This sound was more like a...*HURRICANE!*

Dylan was gasping for air, the blow to her stomach had forced her to the ground. The stranger had followed his tackle with a rapid succession of punches to her ribs, stopping her from inhaling.

Nathan grinned down at her feeling secure in his position atop her body. Flushed with success, he wanted to end this little battle and claim his prize. He looked to his left to see his pistol on the ground near him and he twisted his body to reach for it.

Dylan felt the weight on her stomach shift, relieving some of the tension on her sore ribs. She rolled violently with the shift, throwing the man off of her. She continued the roll and got to her feet just Nathan reached the gun.

Alarmed Dylan knew there was no way she could stop him from reaching the gun in time. She turned, making eye contact with her soulmate. Staggering to her feet she opened her arms just as Lura flew into them.

Lura watched the expression on Dylan's face. She

knew what Dylan was doing, she was saying goodbye and placing her body between herself and the threat, preparing to take the bullet.

Well, she had not spent all her life looking for her lover just to have some ass wipe with a pistol take her away. She dove towards Dylan, wrapping her arms around her lover's waist. She twisted her body, throwing Dylan off balance and effectively switching places with her. Now her back was to Nathan.

As Dylan wrapped her arms around Lura she heard the sound of the gunfire and steeled herself for the impact. She prayed that her body would be able to shield Lura from the bullet. Just as this thought occurred she felt the other woman twist, now Lura's back was to Nathan.

"NO!" Dylan screamed, her eyes wide. Her head lifted as she frantically searched for the lunatic.

Surprised when she did not feel the shudder of a round, Dylan looked up over a blond head and saw the wolf. Its jaws locked around the strange man's throat. The huge wolf had leapt on the man, her massive weight knocking him from his feet. Her teeth were buried deep in the man's throat and she shook her head viciously back and forth, as she would to kill a rat or snake.

Dylan could hear the snap of his neck even over the sound of the wind. Her hair whipped around her face and neck stinging her as it struck out, blinding her and blocking her vision

As the wind picked up, Dylan found it more and more difficult to keep her footing. She had to get them out of this weather. Hugging her soulmate close she glanced back down at her companion and saw the look of terror in Lura's face.

Lura was frightened beyond belief; she had never witnessed a storm like this before. Tears of fear sprang into her eyes and she pulled herself closer to the tall soldier, determined to hold onto her lover. Together they would live or die.

Dylan had no desire to die, she had finally gotten her Falcon back and she was not willing to give her up so quickly. Holding tightly to Lura, she looked around for a place that would shelter them both. Heading to the trees, she saw the flick of a tail and she picked up her pace following the wolf.

Lura held on tightly to the naked waist. She was relieved to be alive, if even for a short time. She feared the storm much more that the bullet. A bullet would have taken her while she lay in Dylan's arms, but the wind of the storms might tear them apart. Fear forced her to turn her head; she stared back at the rapidly disappearing camp. The sight was amazing to watch. The blankets had come to life, flying off into the trees. She looked again noticing for the first time the still body of Nathan Owens near the base of the cedar tree. One large branch had fallen and seemed to have crushed his neck. His eyes were open and his face was a frozen mask of terror.

He must have seen the branch coming, she thought. *What a horrible way to die.* She wrapped her arms tighter around Dylan as she watched the wind begin to lift and twist the body, causing the limbs to dance grotesquely in the air. The large limb that had trapped the dead man's head and neck kept the wind from completely claiming its new toy.

"We have got to find someplace safe," Dylan screamed Lura nodded in agreement, sure that her voice would be carried away by the wind.

186

Dylan led them deeper into the forest towards the hills, finally finding a deep embankment she walked barefoot along it until she came across a small narrow crevasse. She pushed Lura in and followed her. There was just enough room to slide through. They followed the crack in the land to a wide-open overhang. The two women curled up close, facing each other with their legs intertwined.

Dylan wrapped her bare legs tightly around Lura's waist, hoping to prevent the other woman from being captured by the fury of the wind.

They sat together listening to the storm beating the dirt walls of their shelter. Slowly the air stilled, the eye was passing over.

Lura looked up at Dylan, glad to see the fire and anger had left the beautiful face. She had her hero, her Hawk back.

In the stillness of the storm, Lura leaned back into the warm embrace of legs and arms and looked up into the beautiful face, searching for the stress she had seen there earlier. As she looked, her mind finally clicked in and she realized that she was exactly where she wanted to be. No, not in the storm, or the dirt, or the wind, but in the embrace of her lover.

Her heart rate picked up when she realized that they were both alive and Dylan was quite pleasantly naked. The smile on her face grew wider when Dylan looked down into her eyes.

Dylan looked into Lura's smiling face, surprised to see that the look of fear gone, replaced by a silly grin. She was curious.

"Lura? Why are you grinning?"

Lura wiggled an eyebrow, leaned forward and

took a bare nipple in her mouth, tickling it with a warm tongue.

"Lura!" Dylan exclaimed pulling back in surprise. "Woman, we are in the middle of a hurricane and all you can think about is sex?"

"Well, you are right, we are in the hurricane. All the more reason to make love, we may not survive this. I came a very long way to find you Dylan Hawk and if I am going to die, I want to die while making love to the most beautiful woman on this planet."

She leaned forward again this time to accept a pair of willing lips. Her hands slid up and around the warm soft naked body wrapped around hers.

Dylan felt the rough lace of Lura's bra as it scratched her, now alert, sensitive breasts. She felt her inner thighs brush against the silk of Lura's underwear.

"Oh, those have got to go," she mumbled as her fingers worked on the elastic and snaps on the back of the bra. The clasps gave to her strong fingers and she pulled back taking the bra with her. Her fingers now went to work on the underpants.

Lura whimpered with excitement as she felt her breasts freed.

"Dylan, Honey, how are you going to..."

Dylan smiled into Lura's eyes as she stopped her questions with her lips. She took the thin strips of silk in her hands and tore first one side then the other. Placing one strong arm around Lura's waist she lifted the smaller woman off the ground and used the other hand to pull the tattered garment from her body.

Lura gasped when she felt the strong slender fingers slip gently between her legs and stroke her hot flesh. Tightening her legs, she pulled her body closer to Dylan's thrilled when she felt the brush of crisp hair against her groin.

Dylan's fingers slid up and over Lura's hip, her arm tightened around the small waist. She pulled Lura into another deep searching kiss moaning into her mouth when her searching fingers parted moist hair and stroked the trembling bit of flesh she found there. Her fingers moved of their own accord as they felt Lura's clit grow hard.

Lura threw her head back leaning into the embrace of Dylan's legs. She spread her legs wide allowing the cool breeze to brush the moisture that Dylan's still questing fingers created. She watched in fascination as Dylan lifted her fingers to her stare at the slick moisture she had discovered. Smiling the dark woman painted her lips with her fingertips then leaned forward, sharing the taste of Lura's passion, closing her eyes she hummed her appreciation.

Like a starving wolf, Dylan twisted the blond around until her back was to the building wind. She gently lowered Lura to the ground, her eyes caressing every inch of bare flesh she saw.

Lura looked up at a vision she was sure she would remember for the rest of her life. Dylan, her long black hair streaming in the wind looked hungrily at her with deep blue eyes, a gentle smile on her glistening lips.

Slowly Dylan leaned forward, lifting Lura's legs over her shoulders as she bent to take the quivering clit into her mouth, sucking gently. Her fingers slipped deep into Lura, slowly pumping in and out, stroking her walls as they tightened in response.

Feeling Lura near the edge of an orgasm she slowed her hand, and lifted her head. She wanted to see the face of her lover when she came. Slowly she parted the flesh again, her eyes leaving the heavy lidded green ones long enough to glance down at the treasure she had almost lost.

Lura watched in fascination as the dark head bowed, a soft pink tongue slipped from between coral lips and ever so slowly reached down to stroke her clit. As the warm tongue touched her, the blue eyes looked up and a pair of long fingers plunged into her.

Dylan saw the green eyes flutter shut and felt the hard clit quiver in her mouth as a violent shudder passed through the blond curls that warmed her lips. She felt Lura's body shake and she sucked the clit gently between her teeth drawing out the orgasm and the warm flow that followed.

She stilled her fingers as she felt the walls release their hold. Staring again into hooded green eyes she brought her fingers to her lips and slowly licked them clean.

CHAPTER 17

Gray Hawk felt the hard floor beneath his head; the pain in his leg throbbed, forcing him awake. He listened for the sound of the storm but heard nothing. Raising his head he looked out the window and saw the sun shining back at him. He had survived the storm, now if he could just survive the gunshot wounds.

There was a pounding on the front door. He heard voices, but wasn't able to call out. Suddenly the door burst open and his daughter and son-in-law stood in the doorway. John Cameron glanced quickly around taking in the entire room, his eyes settling on the crumpled figure of Gray Hawk on the blood-covered floor.

Dylan felt the small hand in her own and looked over at Lura. She searched the face for signs of fear and found only contentment there. She smiled, her face mirroring that of the naked woman next to her.

She was so preoccupied staring at the smiling face she was taken by surprise by the pinch she felt on her hip.

"Ow!" she exclaimed reaching down to rub the tender place. She turned hurtful eyes to her lover. "What was that for?" she asked with a pouty face that would have done any three year old proud.

"That was for the smug look on your face," Lura said. "And this," she added with a deep kiss, "is for distracting me long enough for the storm to pass. Thank you, sweetheart."

She wrapped her arms around a warm golden tanned waist and buried her face in the silky black hair. She felt a sudden tightening in her chest, her throat closed and she felt her shoulders shake as the tears fell.

"Hey, hey...Lura, what's wrong? Hey the storm is almost gone, you're safe. I promise." Dylan whispered into the fiery gold hair. When she received no response she tightened her hold on the crying woman, a needle of doubt creeping into her mind.

"Lura, are you okay? I...I didn't hurt you did I? Please tell me I didn't hurt you?" She asked holding her breath waiting for the response.

"No" came the broken muffled voice. "I'm fine, I'm better than fine. It's just that first you left me..." she cried, holding tighter to the taller woman. "Then I find you only to cause you pain," she finished softly, the tears slowing.

"No honey, you didn't cause me any pain, if anything, I hurt you. I left you there and ran away like..." She felt a hand cover her lips.

"Listen to me," Lura said wrestling herself up on one arm.

"That man, the one back in the camp. I know him. I brought him here to kill you." She felt Dylan stiffen under her hands.

"What? What do you mean, Lura? You don't

know that guy, do you?" she asked, her heart stopping.

"My mother tried to play match maker. She wanted me to marry Nathan. I tried to get rid of him, but he, he was..."

Dylan could feel the anger rising in the small woman and felt the tension leave her.

"He was like a walking hemorrhoid, a big pain and always on my ass," she said angrily.

Dylan chuckled at the angry blond. Until she felt the hand slap her naked midsection.

"This isn't funny Dylan, Nathan said he hurt your grandfather. He would never have come here if it weren't for me. Don't you see? It's my fault," Lura finished, once again burying her face in the strong shoulder.

Dylan stroked the soft hair, what could she say?

"Lura honey, there is no way that he could have killed my grandfather." Dylan said, "Gray Hawk is the War Chief of my tribe. Your friend Nathan said he cried and begged. Lura, you met my grandfather. Would he have begged for anything?" She felt Lura still; she could almost hear her thinking.

"No, the man I met would never beg," she admitted.

"No, he wouldn't, but I am afraid he may have hurt him. We have to get to the cabin." Dylan said.

As the storm blew itself out the two exhausted women returned to camp to collect what they could of their gear and get dressed. They had expected little of the site to remain and were surprised at what they found. The hut was still standing and relatively untouched, their clothing, shoes and camp gear though tossed about were still there also.

Dylan walked over to check on Nathan he was most defiantly dead, the wind had twisted his body, turning it completely around while the tree limb kept his head pinned in place. He resembled a crumpled doll whose head some mischievous child had tried to twist off.

They left Nathan's corpse where it had fallen.

Dylan turned to Lura hoping that she had not seen the condition of the body.

"That tree limb crushed his throat. It must have been quick." Lura said, her eyes traveling to the broken body.

Dylan started to correct her when she saw the shadow of a large wolf lumber through the edge of the wood line. It paused to turn a silver eyed, wolfish smile her way then continued on to disappear in the shadows.

They dressed quickly then cleaned up the camp, gathering the remainder of their gear. Dylan picked up her tall cedar staff, noticing for the first time the condition of both walking staffs. Both were leaning upright against the large ancient cedar. Both we polished and clean, but the strangest thing was that both now bore the names of totem animals. Dylan's also had the four elements carved into hers. They stared at the staffs, but neither made any comment about the changes. Dylan traced the names wolf and hawk on one portion, earth, wind, fire, and water on another section. She had no idea what it meant but she knew now that the staff her grandfather had always carried was carved the same way.

While Dylan studied the cedar limb, Lura was twisting her staff in her hands amazed at what she saw.

Lura's staff had split in two, the two pieces twisting around each other joining again at the top. The name Badger was etched deeply in the single top portion. She rubbed her thumb over the name and glanced in confusion at Dylan. Dylan simply shook her head with a sigh.

She returned to gathering and loading their packs, as she was anxious to return to the lodge and check on her grandfather.

Hours later two very tired women stumbled from the woods. It was already dark out as they approached the cabin. Dylan had rushed them both out of the forest as quickly as possible considering the conditions in the storm torn forest.

They approached her grandfather's cabin through the clearing. There was no sign of life, no lights on, no smoke from the chimney. Dylan's heart began to pound in fear of what she may find. She slowed as she got closer to the door, her mind flashing back to the mouth of a cave and the broken bloody bodies of her men.

She reached the door, a quick turn of the ancient handle and, nothing, it locked. She leaning her staff against the outer wall, she turned and searching around picked up a large rock. With a twist she opened the rock that was actually a hiding place for a key.

Holding it in her hand she glanced over at a worried Lura.

"Yeah, I know, key in the rock. Hokey. I kept telling him that this was gonna get him..." Dylan felt her throat close on the last words. She turned away to prevent Lura from seeing the tears in her eyes.

Taking the key she slipped it into the lock.

Turning the key she pushed the door open. She smelled a faint, but familiar, metallic smell...blood! She stood in the doorway her feet refusing to move her forward, her body frozen in place.

Lura watched as the color left Dylan's face, her body swaying in the doorway. Dropping her staff, she reached out, wrapping her arms around Dylan's waist, leading her back out onto the porch. She helped the tall woman sit on the front step, forcing her head between her knees. Dylan's mind seemed to have shut down. There were no commands from her brain to her body. She sat gulping lungs full of air, unable to get enough.

A sound finally broke through her haze as a car rolled up the drive with a policeman behind the wheel. Lura stood and walked out to meet the officer, her concern for her partner overriding her initial concern for the old warrior.

Dylan had not moved, her head was still bent and her hands now trembled with anxiety. "Dylan, Dylan honey, the Sheriff is here. He has something to tell you," Lura said.

"Ms. Hawke? Your father sent me, he told me you would be here," the young deputy said. He was not ready for the response he received. The woman, who seemed to be on the edge of collapse transformed before his eyes.

Lura watched in amazement as the deputy began to back peddle, his feet shuffling in the dirt as he tried to escape the charging figure.

Dylan was on her feet in seconds, charging towards the deputy. Grabbing his shirt she lifted him off his feet, her momentum carrying them both back to his sedan. Dylan thrust her arms out slamming the deputy's body into the side of the police sedan.

The eyes staring at him were cold, dead eyes. He saw death there.

"Where is he? Where is my grandfather?" Dylan growled.

The young man broke out in a cold sweat as he stared into the grimacing face of the crazed woman. Dylan had not patience for this and she drew back her fist preparing to get her answers one way or another.

"Wait, wait!" he shouted, holding up a hand to delay the angry brunette.

"That is why I am here, because of your grandfather."

"What about him? Where is he?" she shouted, throwing him against the car again.

"Dylan!" Lura shouted. "Stop, he's trying to tell you. Let him go honey." she asked softly, her hand now resting on the tense arm of the tall angry woman.

Dylan turned her head, confused. She stared down at her lover as if she could not understand what she was saying.

"Ms. Hawke, your father sent me to get you. I'm to take you to your grandfather," the deputy blurted out quickly in the hope of avoiding another jarring impact with the car body.

"What?" Dylan asked. "What did you say?" She stared down at the quivering deputy, her hands finally releasing the young man to land safely back on his feet.

"Grandfather is alright?" she asked

"Yeah, that's what I am trying to tell ya. Your father was here, he found your grandfather wounded in the house. They are at the hospital now. Chief Gray

Hawk is going to be fine. He wants to see you," the deputy said, feeling a bit more confident now that he could breath normally again.

"He said something about bringing the Little Falcon with you." He smiled as he watched the two women shout and hug each other dancing around.

*I guess I can let her go this one time. I probably would feel the same way if it were my Grandad, h*e thought

"Hey, hey!" he shouted, getting the attention of the jubilant women. "You two want to follow me?" He grinned.

Dylan was apprehensive; she hated hospitals, as her experiences with them had been much too long. Even the smell of the floor cleaner brought back unpleasant memories.

"Dylan, Dylan honey? Please, my fingers..." Lura cried.

Her hand was held in Dylan's vice like grip. Her lover had not realized that her grip was crushing the smaller hand.

"Ah, Honey, I'm sorry, it's just that I really don't like hospitals. I just want to see Grandfather," she said turning worried eyes again to the small blond.

Lura rubbed the large slender chilled hand with her own, trying to reassure her lover.

A voice called her name and Dylan looked up to see a tiny woman standing in the doorway. Her uniform informed Dylan that she was a nurse, her nametag read Sarah Heath. She glanced around the room expectantly, waiting for someone to respond.

Dylan sprang to her feet, her eyes bright with anticipation.

"Yes, this is Dylan Hawke," Lura spoke, holding onto Dylan's hand.

"Ah, yes, well, your Grandfather is in room 423. He is asking for you and Little Falcon." If you go down the hall," the nurse pointed. "He is in the third room on the right. Don't keep him up too long, he has been through quite a bit," she warned, shaking a finger at the much taller woman.

"Yes Ma'am," the soldier said, smiling down at the nurse even as her feet began to take her down the long hall, a small blond in tow.

Gray Hawk sat up in bed, his arm in a sling, his leg heavily bandaged.

They had removed the bullets and patched him up and he was ready to go home now. He sat sulking in bed angry that he had been shot and even angrier that he had missed dinner and was forced to spend at least one night in the hospital. Would no one save him from this hell?

The door opened and hope had arrived. His beloved granddaughter walked in with her small soul mate.

Yes, there was hope, he thought, smiling at the concerned look on the soldier's face.

"Dylan, thank the Great Spirit! You have to help me!" he began.

The door opened again and in walked the deputy with a second man in a poorly tailored suit.

"Mr. Hawk?" he asked

"Yes, I am Gray Hawk, and unless you are here to release me from this place of torture, I would like some privacy with my granddaughter," the old man stated.

"Well, I'm sorry Mr. Hawk. I already met Nurse

Heath," he said as he loosened his collar, clearing his throat. "I think that you are out of luck in the escape department

"Mr. Hawk we are here about the incident." The deputy said. "This is Investigator Crosby, he has some questions to ask you about your assailant."

Lura was on her feet in seconds.

"The man who did this was a man named Nathan Owens. He was a stalker looking for me. He is the one who shot Gray Hawk, he told us so. He also tried to kill Dylan," she stated her voice bitter and angry.

The investigator was taking careful notes, writing as fast as he could.

"Miss...?" he asked, looking at the blond questioningly.

"Grant, Lura Gillum-Grant, of the Richmond Grants," Lura stated her voice still angry.

"Miss Grant? You say that a Mr. Owens assaulted Mr. Gray Hawk?" he asked. "What do you base that assumption on?"

"Well, it could be because he bragged about it just before he tried to kill Dylan, Captain Hawk" she said.

"Captain Hawke?" he asked. "The soldier?"

"Yes, the soldier. Owens followed me from Virginia. He was trying to kill Dylan," Lura stated.

"Do you have any idea where we can reach Mr. Owens? We have some questions we would like to ask him," the investigator stated, frowning at the turn of events.

"Yes, he is about three miles west of the cabin, under a large tree branch," Dylan stated quietly staring coldly at the police officers.

"He's dead." Lura added. "He came after us

during the storm. A tree branch fell on him."

The investigator looked up at that staring at first one woman then the other, both meeting his eyes easily. The tall soldier's eyes reflected the pain and strain of the last few hours. He had heard of the Captain and had no doubt that she could have killed the man, but the evidence of the initial assault on the old man led him to believe that the women were telling the truth.

Completing his notes he thanked the women and left them with Gray Hawk.

The old warrior turned puppy dog eyes on his granddaughter. "Dylan, you are my favorite granddaughter. Can't you do something about helping me escape?" he pleaded

Laughing Dylan shook her head, "Grandfather, I am your only granddaughter. If the doctors wants you to stay here, they probably have a very good reason." She grinned.

"That woman, that nurse Heath is a fierce woman. I believe she was a evil shamaness in her last life," he whined.

Lura chuckled knowing that the old warrior was going to have to stay in the hospital and the formidable nurse Heath would have to put up with him until he was released.

As if on cue the door swung open and in walked the tiny nurse.

"Sorry all, but Mr. Hawk needs his rest. You can come and see him tomorrow." She stood, holding the door open waiting impatiently for the two young women to leave.

Laughing, Dylan kissed her grandfather goodbye

and promised to see him the next day.

Lura smiled seeing the same pouting look on Dylan's face before.

They left the room with Dylan walking on air. She was with her soulmate, her grandfather was alive and things were just…

She turned the corner and walked into her father.

CHAPTER 18

For the first time in his career John Cameron was speechless. His daughter was standing in front of him and he had no idea what to say.

"Umm, Hi Dylan. I found Gray Hawk, he's here," he said, stammering like a schoolboy.

Dylan simply looked at him, unsure what to say until Lura jabbed an elbow into her sore side.

"Owwl" she exclaimed, still looking at her father.

"Yeah, thanks. I think you saved his life." She shuffled her feet nervously.

She looked up at her father and smiled nervously.

"Well, that is a start," the Senator said smiling back.

Dylan frowned, "Well, I have things to do. I…I have to go."

Taking Lura's hand Dylan walked around her father and out the front door. She was still not sure if she was ready for a warm fuzzy relationship with the man, but she was willing to give him a chance.

Lura smiled at the broad back, happy to see that

her lover was willing to work on a relationship with her father. She turned and smiled at the Senator.

The silver-haired man smiled back.

The day had been one extreme to the next and the two women were exhausted. Dylan drove the Mercedes back to the cabin. They rode in silence, both women deep in thought. This time when they arrived at the cabin, Dylan was prepared for the smell. What she wasn't prepared for was the note on the front door.

Compliments of Senator John Cameron

They opened the door to the fresh smell of pine. The two women smiled at each other and stumbled off to bed together.

The smell of coffee woke her; she reached over to discover the bed empty but the sheets still warm. Dylan smiled as she rolled over and onto her feet. Checking the clock on the bedside she was surprised to see it was almost one o'clock, they had slept through the morning and most of the afternoon.

She padded barefoot into the kitchen to discover a naked Lura pouring coffee into two tall cups. Dylan leaned against the doorjamb, admiring the view. She was so preoccupied with her favorite past time she was taken by surprise when the soft voice spoke out.

"If you are going to stand there all morning why don't you get the cream out of the frig?" Lura said without looking up.

"How? God, I must be losing my touch. First grandfather now you." Dylan sulked as she strolled into the kitchen and over to the refrigerator. Pulling the door open she leaned forward to retrieve the carton of cream.

Lura stopped pouring long enough to glance up. She smiled as she now took the opportunity to scan her lover's body. The wounds looked almost healed now, she was amazed, and thrilled to know that Dylan would soon be back up to snuff, and she was a happy camper.

"Honey why don't you go take a shower? I have to call my Dad and let him know I'm alright," Lura said.

"Humm, I have a better idea. I will go get in the shower. You finish your coffee and come join me. Then you can call your father." Dylan said, wiggling her eyebrows at Lura as she advanced slowly on the small woman.

Lura laughed backing up slowly, her hands outstretched to hold off the brunette.

"Now Dylan, you know you have been through a lot and you need to rest. Recover your strength," she said, now back peddling.

"Well, what do ya know? I'm HEALED!" Dylan exclaimed grinning from ear to ear while trotting after the nude blond.

Lura giggled and headed for the living room with an equally naked Dylan hot on her trail. She caught the blond in the living room and carried her to the bear fur rug. She made love, slowly, passionately to her falcon, joining their souls.

Dylan woke up for the second time that day, rolled in a bearskin rug. "Lura? Lura?" she called, walking through the house dragging the large rug wrapped around her.

She entered the bedroom that they had shared only hours before. There on the bed was a blue satin gown, matching pumps and a velvet box lay next to it. There was a note by her pillow along with the keys to the Benz.

My love,
   I am waiting at the Sterling Swan.
Lura.

Dylan entered the restaurant feeling very vulnerable. It had been quite a while since she had worn anything as beautiful as the blue gown.

She stared around the room trying to spot a small blond. A maître d' in a black tuxedo approached.

"Ms. Hawke, your party is waiting. Would you please follow me?" he said weaving his way around table after table.

Surprised and curious Dylan was unaware of the admiring glances she was receiving.

The soldier did not resemble a soldier this evening. Her elegant body was wrapped in a dark blue gown. Its clever construction teased the eye of the admirer with a tantalizing glimpse of bare thigh as the tall brunette walked. Her silky black hair was twisted into an intricate knot at the back of her head, tendrils escaping to caress her cheeks.

Long, golden legs looked even longer in the beautiful three-inch sling back heels. A single strand of glowing white pearls accentuated the graceful neck.

Dylan was seated alone at a table next to the dance floor. She shifted uncomfortably in her chair, glancing around at the other patrons, all couples.

She was ready to leave when she felt a hand on her shoulder and she glanced up to see Lura. Her lover was dressed in a sleek red dress, the back cut low and the front high. She looked beautiful, expensive and off limits.

Sliding into the chair across from Dylan she nodded to the waiter who stepped forward and lit the single candle on the table. Lura watched as Dylan's eyes glittered in the flickering flame. The waiter returned moments later with a bottle of chilled wine. He poured a bit into a glass and waited while Lura first tasted it then nodded her head. Filling both glasses he disappeared.

Neither woman spoke they sipped their wine as the waiter returned again with two plates of food. Dylan raised a brow as a large steak filet with corn, French cut beans and hot bread was placed in front of her. The steak was warm and rare, the wine was chilled and Dylan was enjoying herself. Lura had not spoken a word she simply watched as Dylan slowly consumed her meal. Dylan was enjoying the game; Lura was flirting without saying a word.

They finished their meal and sat sipping the last of the wine. Dylan was anxious to continue this game back at home.

She was very surprised then as the lights dimmed and the music softened. Lura smiled as she watched the blue eyes grow large then narrow as they turned to look at her.

"Lura, what are you up to?" she asked, a smile on

her lips.

She stood and held out her hand to the surprised Dylan.

"Dance with me, Hawke."

Dylan slipped her hand into Lura's and allowed her to lead her to the dance floor.

She followed the beautiful blonde, glaring at the disapproving looks they were receiving.

No one seemed to want to challenge the dark haired woman.

They reached the center of the floor and she wrapped her arms around Lura's small waist and pulled her close, closing her eyes to enjoy the feel of the woman she loved swaying with the music.

Behind the two women a silent screen lowered, as romantic scenes of sunsets and beaches played behind them.

As the music slowed Lura raised her hand to signal the maître d' again. The music changed as a single guitarist stepped out onto the stage. She seated herself on a stool and began to play, singing along softly along with the music.

Would you dance
if I asked you to dance?
Would you run
and never look back?
Would you cry
if you saw me cry?
And would you save my soul, tonight?

The screen behind the two women darkened, the scenes on the screen changed. No longer were there pictures of sunsets. Instead the screen darkened with the image of endless sand. A helicopter flew in landing and stirring up the powdery sand. A camera zoomed in once the helicopter landed. Troops poured out, rifles at the ready. They charged the enemy and in the background flashes of gunfire lit a mountain cave.

Would you tremble
if I touched your lips?
Would you laugh?
Oh please tell me this.
Now would you die
for the one you loved?
Hold me in your arms, tonight.

I can be your hero, baby.
I can kiss away the pain.
I will stand by you forever.
You can take my breath away.

The picture switched to a stretcher, a wounded soldier covered in blood was hustled onto the helicopter through a whirl of dust.

Would you swear
that you'll always be mine?
Or would you lie?
would you run and hide?

Am I in too deep?
Have I lost my mind?
I don't care...
You're here tonight.

A small distraught blond, her face covered in dirt, her hand covered in blood ran after the stretcher, tears streaking her face. She fought against the arms holding her, keeping her away from the soldier.

I can be your hero, baby.
I can kiss away the pain.
I will stand by you forever.
You can take my breath away.

Oh, I just want to hold you.
I just want to hold you.
Am I in too deep?
Have I lost my mind?
I don't care...
You're here tonight.

The other diners watched stunned as the next shot showed the same soldier, her face battered and bruised with her head thrown back in a silent scream of pain as she struggled to walk.

I can be your hero, baby.
I can kiss away the pain.
I will stand by your forever.
You can take my breath away.

The slide show continued with picture after picture of a warrior's struggle, ending with the presentation of the Medal of Honor from the President of the United States.

I can be your hero.
I can kiss away the pain.
And I will stand by you forever.
You can take my breath away.

As the final notes of the song faded the lights came up and Dylan looked around. For the first time she realized that they were alone on the dance floor. She glanced around to see every person in the restaurant on their feet.

She heard the murmur of her name as the crowd broke into applause. Too stunned to speak she felt a tug on her hand and turned to see Lura down on one knee.

"Lura? What? What are you doing? Get up, people are staring," Dylan whispered pulling at Lura's arm.

"Dylan I love you, shut up," Lura said in frustration. There was soft laughter from the now staring crowd.

"Now, where was I? Oh yeah. Dylan Hawk, I love you. I have loved you since the day I met you. Would you please be my life-mate?

Dylan pulled Lura to her feet, brushing her blond hair behind her ear as she smiled into the beautiful green eyes.

"There is one thing you have to remember, Little Falcon. The mate of the Hawk never has to beg."

The crowd applauded as the couple in the center of the floor sealed their promise with a kiss.

The end, until the next time.

About the Author

CPT Katherine E. Standell
US Army Military Police Corp

Katherine E. Standell is from a strong military family. The family history with the military goes back some four generations, with members of her immediate family in both the Army and the Air Force. Her father, a Korean War veteran has several awards including a Purple Heart, the Bronze Star with two oak leaf clusters and a Legion of Merit, which is the highest possible peace time award for service above and beyond the call of duty. It is second only to the Medal of Honor.

A graduate of Pembroke State University, Ms. Standell has an Undergraduate degree in Education and a Masters in Administration, however she felt compelled to join the military upon completion of school and has enjoyed the challenges the service has offered.

Born and raised in the Carolinas, Katherine loves the outdoors and spends much of her free time with her Husky/Wolf mix trekking the high trails of the Blue Ridge Mountains.

Katherine served in the military for nearly ten years before injuries suffered while on duty forced her to leave. A highly trained Military Police Officer, her areas of expertise include Counter Terrorism and Personal Security. Presently, she is looking forward to retirement and hopes to have the opportunity to complete several more stories in the Hawk and Falcon Series as well as two additional books with new characters.

Limitless D2D	Order Form	
The Amazon Queen By L M Townsend	20.00	
Define Destiny By J M Dragon	20.00	
Desert Hawk, revised By Katherine E. Standell	18.00	
Golden Gate By Erin Jennifer Mar	18.00	
The Brass Ring By Mavis Applewater	18.00	
Paradise Found By Cruise and Stoley	20.00	
Spirit Harvest By Trish Shields	15.00	
Omega's Folly By Carla Osborne	12.00	
Up The River-out of print **...While supplies last...** By Sam Ruskin	15.00	
Memories Kill By S. B. Zarben	20.00	
Connecting Hearts By Val Brown and M. J. Walker	18.00	
	Total	

South Carolina residents add 5% sales tax.
Domestic shipping is $3.50 per book
Visit our website at: http://limitlessd2d.net
Please mail your orders with a check or money order
to:

Limitless, Dare 2 Dream Publishing
100 Pin Oak Ct.
Lexington, SC 29073

Please make checks or money orders payable to:
Limitless Corporation

Limitless D2D	Order Form	
Shattering Rainbows By Ocean	18.00	
Kara: Lady Rogue By j. taylor Anderson	18.00	
Mysti: Mistress of Dreams By Sam Ruskin	18.00	
Indiscretions By Cruise	18.00	
A Thousand Shades of Feeling By Carolyn McBride	16.00	
The Amazon Nation **By Carla Osborne**	20.00	
Poetry from the Featherbed By pinfeather	18.00	
Encounters, Book I By Anne Azel	22.00	
Encounters, Book II By Anne Azel	25.00	
The Fellowship By K. Darblyne	18.00	
Deadly Rumors By Jeanne Foguth	20.00	
	Total	

South Carolina residents add 5% sales tax.
Domestic shipping is $3.50 per book
Visit our website at: http://limitlessd2d.net
Please mail your orders with a check or money order to:

Limitless, Dare 2 Dream Publishing
100 Pin Oak Ct.
Lexington, SC 29073

Please make checks or money orders payable to:
Limitless Corporation

Limitless D2D	Order Form	
Cat on the Couch By Cathy L. Parker	16.00	
Commitments By Cruise	18.00	
Up The River, Revised By Sam Ruskin	18.00	
Return of the Warrior By Katherine E. Standell	18.00	
Haunting Shadows By J M Dragon	18.00	
A Saving Solace By D S Bauden	18.00	
Passion's Phrases By Charlsie Todd	15.00	
Perhaps by Chance By K. Stoley	18.00	
Port of Call By K. Stoley	18.00	
PWP: Plot, What Plot? By Mavis Applewater	18.00	
Queen's Lane By I. Christie/J A Bard	18.00	
	Total	

South Carolina residents add 5% sales tax.
Domestic shipping is $3.50 per book
Visit our website at: http://limitlessd2d.net
Please mail your orders with a check or money order to:

Limitless, Dare 2 Dream Publishing
100 Pin Oak Ct.
Lexington, SC 29073

Please make checks or money orders payable to:
Limitless Corporation

Claire	While You Sleep	Always Forever	Morning Coffee	The Bite
All For You	Female Beauty	Loved	Bubblebath	Mine

	Perfection	Your Love	
			My Love
Mirror			
	Think of You	With You	Your Eyes
		Together	By My Side
			Mmmmm

Unless otherwise specified the cards will come blank, with no printing inside. You may, however, request something be printed inside at no extra cost.